Adventures of **Vicky** and **Tej**

THE
HAUNTED
LAKE

Siddharth Borker

Chennai • Bangalore

CLEVER FOX PUBLISHING
Chennai, India

Published by CLEVER FOX PUBLISHING 2025
Copyright © Siddharth Borker 2025

All Rights Reserved.
ISBN: 978-93-67077-23-8

This book has been published with all reasonable efforts taken to make the material error-free after the consent of the author. No part of this book shall be used, reproduced in any manner whatsoever without written permission from the author, except in the case of brief quotations embodied in critical articles and reviews.

The Author of this book is solely responsible and liable for its content including but not limited to the views, representations, descriptions, statements, information, opinions and references ["Content"]. The Content of this book shall not constitute or be construed or deemed to reflect the opinion or expression of the Publisher or Editor. Neither the Publisher nor Editor endorse or approve the Content of this book or guarantee the reliability, accuracy or completeness of the Content published herein and do not make any representations or warranties of any kind, express or implied, including but not limited to the implied warranties of merchantability, fitness for a particular purpose. The Publisher and Editor shall not be liable whatsoever for any errors, omissions, whether such errors or omissions result from negligence, accident, or any other cause or claims for loss or damages of any kind, including without limitation, indirect or consequential loss or damage arising out of use, inability to use, or about the reliability, accuracy or sufficiency of the information contained in this book.

Contents

Acknowledgements .... *vii*
Disclaimer .... *ix*
Prologue .... *xi*

1. The Road Trip 1
2. The Tour of Ganeshpuri 11
3. The Lake 18
4. The Investigation Begins 23
5. The Night Watch 35
6. At the Brick Factory 43
7. The Headless Boatman! 59
8. A Visit to Ganeshpuri Railway Station 64
9. Observation Deck 70
10. Close Encounters 97
11. The Cave 104
12. Beyond the Waterfall 109
13. All that Glitters is Gold! 115
14. Final Showdown 121
15. The Unmasking Ceremony 134
16. Connecting the Dots 138
17. Goodbye Ganeshpuri! 154

Acknowledgements

This book would not have been possible without the support and encouragement of several remarkable people, to whom I am deeply grateful.

First and foremost, my heartfelt thanks go to my family. To my wife, Deviya, for her unwavering belief in my potential as a writer. Her faith in me and her persistent encouragement were the driving forces behind this project. Without her, this book might have remained just a dream.

To my son, Anurag, who was not only the first to hear my story but also provided invaluable feedback that helped me get started—your insights shaped the foundation of this work. In addition, Anurag's technical expertise was instrumental in navigating the complexities of electronic publishing, making sure the eBook version reached readers smoothly.

I am also immensely grateful to Rithvik Jaishanker, a gifted young artist, and the son of my dear friend Jai Shanker Bhoothanath (Jai). Rithvik, currently pursuing his bachelor's degree in graphic design at MIT ID Indore,

Avantika University, designed the stunning front cover of this book. I have watched his artistic journey from childhood, and his immense talent continues to amaze me. Thank you, Rithvik, for taking time out of your academic commitments to create a design that truly captures the essence of this book—making it one that readers can indeed judge by its cover.

Lastly, I extend my deepest gratitude to my longtime friends and colleagues, Sridhar Nagabhushana and Jai Bhoothanath. For over two decades, our friendship has been a source of strength and inspiration. As beta readers and critics, your honest, unbiased feedback was instrumental in shaping the final manuscript. You both took this book to heights I hadn't imagined, and for that, I thank you.

Disclaimer

This book is a work of fiction. While certain elements may be inspired by real events, the narrative, characters, names, places, events, and incidents portrayed in this book are purely the product of the author's imagination. Any resemblance to actual persons, living or deceased, or to real events or locations, is purely coincidental.

This book does not promote or endorse the use of alcohol, tobacco, drugs, firearms, explosives, or any other harmful substances or objects.

The content of this book is intended solely for entertainment and does not encourage risky or harmful behavior.

Furthermore, the book does not intend to offend, misrepresent, or malign any religion, race, gender, ethnic group, organization, belief system, culture, ritual, or tradition.

The author and contributors bear no responsibility for any interpretations beyond the intended purpose of entertainment and leisurely reading.

Prologue

*I*n this gripping and mysterious adventure, cousins Vicky and Tej, along with their loyal dog, Chatur, visit their childhood friend Tanmay in the eerie village of Ganeshpuri.

Tej, son of Nishant Kamat, a high-ranking decorated officer in the Indian Intelligence Wing, and his cousin Vicky, adopted by the Kamat family, grew up immersed in the world of covert operations and intelligence work.

Chatur, their ever alert and loyal companion, is a retired Belgian Malinois from the Indian Army, adopted by the Kamats after his service. Though retired, he remains fit, strong, and highly intelligent, making him an invaluable part of their team.

Right on their first day at Ganeshpuri, they hear chilling stories about the village lake, said to be haunted by the headless ghost of Anna. Villagers claim to have seen the ghost and speak of people who ventured to the far side of the lake, never to return.

Intrigued yet skeptical, Tej and Vicky, armed with their investigative skills and accompanied by Chatur, decide to uncover the truth behind the hauntings. As they dig deeper into the mystery, eerie occurrences and mounting suspense make them question whether they are dealing with something supernatural or more sinister forces at play.

Will they solve the mystery, or will the lake's dark secrets consume them too? Prepare for a spine-tingling journey as Tej and Vicky face their first adventure mystery!

1

The Road Trip

"We should be there in an hour! I just can't wait!" Tej said excitedly, hands on the wheel as they drove to Ganeshpuri, their school friend Tanmay's hometown.

Vicky didn't seem to pay attention. He was deeply engrossed in the natural beauty of the western ghats as their Mahindra Thar navigated through the winding roads in between the mountains.

The rainy season had just kicked off. The entire terrain had turned green, and trees were thickly populated with lush green leaves, coupled with seasonal waterfalls in the distant hills. The tree-lined roads made the entire environment even more breathtaking! As they climbed up the ghats, they noticed a reasonable drop in temperature.

The roads were not so kind, though. Heavy rains during the past few days had carved out numerous potholes of various shapes and sizes. Tej had to skillfully navigate around those, which he did very well indeed!

But all that twists and turns game to dodge the potholes was much easier in the best-in-class jeep he was driving.

Tejas (Tej) and Vikrant (Vicky), both twenty-three, were cousins who shared a close, brotherly bond. When Vicky lost both his parents at the age of five, Tej's parents took him in, raising him with the same love and care as their own son.

Tej appeared lean and fit while Vicky was a little plumper, more so because of the kind of glutton he was! Whenever he saw food, he would act as though he hadn't eaten for ages!

Tej was a serious and analytical type, with a natural affinity for technology. Hand him any gadget, and he'd have it figured out within minutes. His skills extended to unlocking any lock or safe—whether mechanical or digital—making him expert in the tech space.

Vicky, on the other hand, was more of a happy-go-lucky character. Whatever the situation, the sarcasm inside him refused to leave.

Tej's father, Nishant Kamat, worked for the Indian Intelligence Wing. He was a top-notch decorated officer and had received several medals for his achievements. He had led many covert operations as well as peacetime rescue missions both within and beyond Indian borders.

Over the years, his qualities had rubbed on to Tej and Vicky. They had the experience of assisting him informally on various occasions. He had trained them to respond to any danger and deal with extremely vulnerable situations.

Both were athletic, martial arts professionals, avid swimmers, and happened to be much stronger for their age.

They were in the final year of a four-year engineering degree program but had a keen interest in becoming private investigators.

The 4WD SUV they possessed was gifted to them by Nishant for scoring well in their engineering entrance exams and acquiring admission to one of the top engineering colleges in Mumbai three years ago.

They had modified it internally with special compartments to suit their needs. It was equipped with mountaineering equipment, swimming gear, semi-knocked-down (SKD) kits of mountain bikes, surveillance equipment, among numerous other things, and a small arms and ammunition compartment as well. It was an 'adventure-ready' beast.

The back seat was left empty for their partner Chatur!

Chatur the dog was a Belgian Malinois who had served the Indian Army in various covert operations as well as peaceful missions. His near-black hair made him almost invisible in the dark.

After about three years, the army had to cut short his service as he did not meet the required fitness criteria. Thereafter, the Kamat family decided to adopt him.

Although not in the army anymore, Chatur was faster, more intelligent, and stronger than any ordinary guard dog. He could sniff out narcotics, explosives, and humans trapped under debris. Chatur dogged bullets like a pro. In all the covert operations he participated in, he was not hit even once!

The Kamat brothers could see the Ganeshpuri railway platform about a hundred meters away.

"Here we are finally!" Vicky said, his voice full of excitement.

Tej noticed the signboard and steered the jeep to the left onto a narrower but neatly tarred road.

Vicky's cell phone started ringing. It was Tanmay! "Hey, Vicky! Where have you guys reached? Don't miss my house near the village entrance, on the left-hand side! I am standing right at the gate!" Vicky heard an excited Tanmay at the other end of the cell phone.

Vicky replied excitedly, "Will be with you in about a minute, buddy!"

Moments later, Tej and Vicky could see Tanmay waving his hands with a big smile on his face.

The jeep came to a screeching halt at the gate! They greeted each other with a high five, happy to meet again.

No sooner he saw Tanmay, Chatur jumped out of the vehicle and pounced on him, almost knocking him to the ground with a loud woof. He hadn't forgotten his old friend and began licking his face excitedly. Vicky had to catch hold of his collar and pull him back!

Tanmay escorted them into his home, where his parents, Mr. Vilasrao Patil and Mrs. Shanta Patil were waiting to welcome them.

Mr. Vilasrao was a tall, well-built gentleman with a wheatish complexion. He sported a thick moustache and 'salt and pepper' hair. He wore a silk kurta and lehenga (a traditional Indian dress quite common in rural India) and Kolhapuri chappals (decorative handcrafted and braided leather slippers that originated from Kolhapur in Maharashtra state).

He was a prominent figure in the village and had been elected as Sarpanch — Village Head who leads the village council, on multiple occasions. His repeated elections reflected the respect and trust he commanded within the community, as well as his dedication to the village's welfare.

Tanmay's mother was slightly shorter and lighter-skinned than her husband and a little plump. She was dressed in a pure silk saree with a mangalsutra (a gold chain with black beads worn by married Hindu women in India), minimal jewelry, and a big bindi (a decorative mark worn in the middle of the forehead by married Indian women, especially Hindus) and carried a sweet, welcoming smile on her face.

"Ah, so you've finally arrived!" she exclaimed with a warm smile, her eyes lighting up. "Tanmay, please show them to their room and make sure they're comfortable." She turned towards the Kamat brothers. "I'm sure after that long drive, you're both starving! Lunch will be ready soon, and I've prepared a special meal just for you," She paused for a moment, looking at them fondly. "It's so good to have you here!"

Then, noticing Chatur, her smile grew even warmer. She bent down and patted him affectionately. "And you must be Chatur! How wonderful to see you too! I've got the finest pedigree treat waiting, just for you. You're going to love it!"

Chatur wagged his tail, clearly pleased by the attention, and responded with a mild woof. Though he appreciated the warm welcome, he wasn't overly friendly, as he was meeting her for the first time.

"Welcome to our village!" Tanmay's father greeted them with a warm, welcoming smile. "I'm sure you'll enjoy your stay here—there's something truly special about the peace and simplicity of village life." With a nod, he signaled to his servants to bring in their luggage.

"Please, make yourselves at home. If there's anything you need, don't hesitate to ask. We're so glad to have you with us!" his voice was full of warmth and hospitality.

The Kamat brothers had an instant comfortable, homely feeling after meeting Tanmay's parents.

The house was huge, with numerous rooms and a 'Razangan'—an open-to-sky space at the center of the house. This style of architecture is a hallmark of traditional homes in the Konkan region of Maharashtra, India.

They could see some posh rooms constructed slightly away but still within the compound of the property. The rooms were tastefully designed, blending modern amenities with the rustic charm of the surroundings.

Tanmay pointed out, "Those are homestays for visiting tourists." He explained that his village was popular among travellers who sought a peaceful retreat in the area.

As they walked out of the living room, into a passage, the sound of birds and rustling leaves filled the air, adding to the serenity of the place. It led them to a large wooden door at the back of the main house, where they were greeted by a tall, dark-skinned, clean-shaven man in his early thirties—well-built and friendly. Tanmay introduced him as Tukya, a short name for Tukaram.

With a polite smile, Tukya gestured for them to follow. He was accompanied by a couple of servants, who had already brought their luggage in and were standing nearby. Tanmay walked alongside Tukya, chatting casually, while the others followed in silence, enjoying the quiet surroundings of the estate.

Once the Kamat brothers were settled in their room, Tanmay gave them a cheerful smile. "Well, freshen up and get ready for lunch," he said. "I've planned a little village tour for you right after that!" With a friendly nod, he stepped out, giving Tej and Vicky some space to settle in and unwind after their long journey.

The room was spacious, extending into a large balcony nearly half its size, with an attached washroom.

At the center stood a huge bed with a ceiling fan overhead. Beside the bed, a large writing table with an overhead reading light offered a cozy workspace. A four-door wardrobe occupied the space next to the table, while a huge couch, almost the size of a single bed, sat in the corner directly opposite the bed.

"Super room, but no air conditioning?" Vicky remarked, glancing around at the antique, traditional decor. Then he added with a smile, "Actually, with this cool weather, I don't think we'd even need it."

Tej chuckled, giving his brother a playful look. "Well, we've got one in the bedroom back in Mumbai, right? I guess we just can't live without it in the city!"

Vicky grinned, nodding in agreement. "True! I wish the weather in Mumbai was like this. It's so much cooler and fresher here—it's like a whole different world!"

Tej leaned back, taking a deep breath of the crisp village air. "Yeah, I could get used to this. It's amazing how the simple things, like fresh air and quiet mornings, make such a difference."

Vicky stretched, looking out the window. "I think I'll sleep like a baby here," he said, then added, "Everything feels so calm."

Tej smiled, nodding. "Exactly. It's the perfect escape from the chaos of the city."

After unpacking their luggage and putting their clothes into the wardrobes, the Kamat brothers decided to take a quick, warm shower to shake off the travel fatigue.

Refreshed and relaxed, they settled down for a short nap, eager to recharge before the village tour Tanmay had planned for the afternoon.

2
The Tour of Ganeshpuri

*I*t was about four o'clock in the afternoon. Tej and Vicky were all set for the village tour after a very heavy lunch of assorted dishes made from fish and chicken, followed by afternoon tea.

Tanmay was at the wheels in his open jeep. Threatening clouds could be seen at a distance, predicting some heavy showers later in the evening. It was overcast and cool, with no sign of immediate rain. A light breeze cooled their faces. It was just the weather they hoped for!

Tej sat next to Tanmay, and Vicky made himself comfortable beside Chatur in the back seat.

As they navigated the small but neatly paved roads, they could see numerous well-built, meticulously planned houses lined up, each having a large backyard full of fruit-bearing trees, vegetables, greenhouses, etc.

They spotted a primary health center, a primary school, a post office, a small police station, a couple of cafes, a community hall, a small market area, and a chapel as well. The village seemed to have pretty much everything!

"Villagers in Ganeshpuri are very self-sufficient. Around a hundred families! All grow vegetables and fruits they need in their backyard, and some are into fishing," Tanmay said proudly as he steered his jeep slowly on the village roads. "Most have converted a part of their home into a homestay. You will find local as well as international tourists over the weekend."

On the top of a hill, they spotted a beautiful temple made of marble. It was quite big and impressive. It was not something that one would expect in such a small village. The Kamat brothers could hear the temple bells ringing from down below.

"That's our Ganesha temple; the village was named after it. It is more than a hundred years old. The original temple was a small structure built by our forefathers, while the one you see now is only about fifteen years old. It houses the same old Ganesha idol," Tanmay said. "There is a motorable road that can take you up there. We shall pay a visit during your stay here."

The Kamat brothers were pleasantly surprised to see solar streetlights lining both sides of every road!

"A model village indeed, much ahead in time!" Tej declared with admiration.

"Now I will take you to the best attraction of my village, our lake!" Tanmay said. He took a sharp turn to join another road. Huge trees dotted the road on either side.

After a few minutes, they could see glimpses of sparkling, crystal-clear, blue lakebed behind the thick trees on the left-hand side.

Moments later, they reached the banks of the lake. It was much larger than it appeared from behind the trees! It was so big that the far side of the lake could hardly be seen! They could also hear a waterfall!

"At the far side, about a kilometer from here, the lake flows into a small waterfall," said Tanmay. "You should be able to get a better view when we visit the temple. A part of it is visible from the top of the hill."

The near side of the lake boasted a small but beautifully constructed jetty adjoining a small, well-maintained garden with sit-outs facing the lake. At the jetty, about a dozen small, motorized fishing boats were neatly anchored side by side, their vibrant colors reflecting off the calm water.

A small lakeside restaurant with a large board, 'Lake View Inn' caught their attention. It appeared to be more of a cozy cafe with a fishing deck and a few rooms. The scenery was picture-perfect.

They parked the jeep, strolled around a bit, and had a few selfies clicked.

"Let's go to the cafe." Tanmay pointed out to the 'Lake View Inn' and walked towards it. Vicky, Tej, and Chatur followed. They walked up to the fishing deck, occupied the sit-outs, and ordered some tea and chicken sandwiches. Chatur curled up at their feet.

As they munched on the chicken sandwiches and sipped hot tea, Tej and Tanmay talked about their school days, laughing over old memories and sharing stories of their mischievous adventures, while Chatur happily enjoyed his share.

Vicky was all about the sandwiches, acting like they were the best thing ever. He nodded vaguely at what Tej and Tanmay were talking about, his mouth full as he gobbled down a couple. Clearly, he was more interested in eating than in the conversation!

Time passed quickly, and it was almost seven in the evening. The sun had begun to set, casting a dark orange glow across the sky. The lake, now calm and still, reflected the changing colors. The water's surface glowed as the light faded, and shadows crept over the edges. The mist rising from the lake made everything feel quiet and a little mysterious.

Tanmay glanced at his wristwatch. "Oh no!" he gasped, his voice trembling with sudden panic. "I—I didn't realize it was so late! Let's go back!"

He jumped up from his seat, his heart racing, and hurried toward the hotel counter to make the payment, his footsteps fast and uneven. "We need to get home before it gets dark!" he said, his voice strained, panic in every word. "We shouldn't stay here a moment longer!"

"What's the hurry? We are here for a vacation anyway! What's waiting for us at home?" Tej asked, astonished.

Tanmay seemed in no mood to hear anything. "Let's get back home, and then I will tell you everything," he said as he hurried back to his jeep.

The Kamat brothers looked at each other, surprise written clearly in their eyes.

Sometime ago, everything looked so fine. "What's happened to Tanmay?" they wondered.

As they rushed back, they could see the 'Lake View Inn' owner hurriedly pulling down the shutters and calling it a day.

"Why is he shutting down so early? It's barely seven in the evening! What's happening?" they wondered as they continued to follow Tanmay without asking any further questions.

The village, which had felt so welcoming, now seemed to hold some dark secrets. The once charming streets now appeared quiet, and the air carried an unsettling stillness.

Chatur sensed the urgency, raced past them and jumped onto the back seat.

Tanmay raced the jeep like he was in an off-road rally through the Himalayas, not saying a word, his foot heavy on the accelerator. It was nearly dark, the sky a deep purple. The headlights cut through the streets, casting long shadows. Light drizzle tapped on the windshield as they sped through the winding road.

Chatur liked the rain. He was enjoying the ride. But his enjoyment was short-lived as Tanmay managed to reach home in record time. His jeep came to a screeching halt in his garage.

He jumped out of the vehicle, called everyone in, and shut the main door, as if something or someone was following him.

The Kamat brothers had a lot of questions swirling in their minds.

As they walked into the living room, irresistible aroma of chicken curry and fresh butter naans (Indian flatbread) pulled them away from their thoughts momentarily.

"Wow, this smells delicious!" Vicky exclaimed, his mouth watering, and his tongue almost out, at the sight of dishes laid out on the dining table. Having already digested the sandwiches, he was ready for more.

They washed their hands and joined others at the dinner table and saved their questions for later.

3

The Lake

*S*oon after dinner, Tej and Vicky joined Tanmay on his massive, beautiful terrace. It had old antique chairs on one side under a gazebo, with a small wall garden facing it. They made themselves comfortable in those chairs.

"Okay, so what's this all about? Why did we rush back?" Tej inquired with an intense stare at Tanmay. "Even that 'Lake View Inn' cafe owner was pulling down the shutters!"

Tanmay sat next to them, took a deep breath, and looked at them. The Kamat brothers could sense fear in his eyes. "Where do I even begin?" he murmured, his voice heavy. "I didn't want to drag you into all of this. You're here to relax and enjoy your vacation, but I can't leave you with unanswered questions."

"Guys, believe me or not, the lake is haunted! No one wanders out in the open anywhere near it after dark! And anyone who dares to go to the far side, I mean, near the waterfall at night, either by boat or along the bank, is never seen again!"

"About two years ago, a couple of tourists decided to visit the far side at night and never returned. The police, assisted by the villagers, searched the lake and the jungle area beyond the waterfall the very next morning but didn't find them! They just disappeared without a trace! Even the local police avoid crossing over to the far side after dark since that incident."

"What about their belongings? Did anyone inquire about them?" Tej asked.

"Well, no one, and they're still in the storeroom of the homestay where they were staying," Tanmay replied. "Since the police didn't find any clues, they closed the case a few months later."

Tanmay looked at the Kamat brothers. "And it doesn't end here!" He paused, took a deep breath, and continued, "At times during misty or stormy nights, people have spotted a boat on the far side of the lake, navigated by a headless boatman with a lantern in his hand! Those who have witnessed this say the boat lingers for a few minutes before vanishing into thin air!"

"At first, we thought someone from the village might be up to some mischief. But when we checked, it wasn't any of the boats owned by the villagers. The boat they saw was much bigger, more like a passenger boat. The locals here own small fishing boats, like the ones you saw when we visited the lake. Some have small paddle boats as well, which tourists hire on an hourly basis. That's all there is to it!"

Tej and Vicky had heard the unexpected! They didn't know what to say!

Tanmay's father overheard this conversation and joined them. "About fifty years ago, there was a man who owned a boat. He was a fisherman but also ferried tourists to the far side of the lake, at the edge of the waterfall, to earn some extra money. We called him Anna (A respectful term for an elder brother in Maharashtra and South India)," he paused, casting a serious glance at Vicky and Tej. "One day, some tourists requested him to take them to the far end at night. They promised him a higher fare, and even though the weather forecast was not favorable for venturing out in the waters, he agreed instantly. Some villagers warned him, but he chose to ignore them."

"Anna struggled to make both ends meet. He just couldn't resist the money he was promised. Despite the risk, he happily welcomed them on board."

"As the boat was about to reach the waterfall, it came under a cloudburst! The sheer force was too much—the boat couldn't take it and went out of control! It hit a rock or something and capsized. All passengers, including Anna and his crew, did not survive."

"During those times we neither had fast boats nor the equipment to conduct rescue operations in quick time. We tried our best but failed! I was just about ten years old then. This is all that I can remember."

"Although I have never seen this Anna myself, people talk about him and claim to have seen him sitting in the boat, with a lantern, without his head! Just the neck and nothing above! With blood oozing from the open wound!" He paused for a moment and continued, "Have fun while you are here. Ganeshpuri is a nice place! Just stay away from the lake. You're our guests, and I want you to stay safe."

The air was thick with tension as they absorbed his words. The eerie image of the headless man lingered in their minds, and the weight of the conversation seemed to hang in the air for a moment.

It was almost midnight. Tanmay's father, noticing their stunned silence, gently suggested that the Kamat brothers get some rest.

Back in their room, their minds started racing as they lay on their bed trying to catch some sleep. Both were still getting goosebumps!

They were tired after the road trip and the village tour that followed, but all that they just heard couldn't let them sleep.

"What a hair-raising tale! Is this real? Would you believe what we just heard?" Vicky said, staring at the blank, whitewashed ceiling as he relaxed on his bed.

"I don't want to completely rule out paranormal possibilities. Some things in the world are beyond human knowledge and understanding," Tej said. "Headless Boatman! Blood oozing out of the neck! My God! Good enough to give anyone a heart attack!"

"Yup!" Vicky agreed. "It looks like it's right out of a Ramsay Brothers horror movie."

All this while the Kamat brothers assisted their father on his assignments. This was their first opportunity to solve a mystery on their own, and one that involved a headless ghost!

4

The Investigation Begins

*T*ej and Vicky could hardly catch any sleep that night. Their minds were preoccupied with all kinds of questions.

The next morning, they were at the breakfast table munching some hot Kanda Pohe (a popular breakfast dish from Maharashtra made from beaten rice) and sipping at some good fresh filter coffee.

Vicky turned towards Tanmay. "Tanmay, since when have the villagers been seeing this headless boatman and his boat?" he inquired.

Tanmay said, "Well, it started about four years ago. Villagers believe that Anna is seeking revenge because they did not save him and his crew back then. He has returned to make them pay for the mistakes of their past. Every weekend, a prayer held at the Ganesha temple, asking for protection from Anna's vengeance."

The room went quiet for a moment as they continued their breakfast, letting his words settle. Outside, the day was slowly coming to life. The faint sounds of the village echoed through the open windows—children laughing as they hurried to school, and the distant clatter of pots from the kitchen.

The soft murmur of neighbors exchanging morning greetings in Marathi, the local language. 'Kay bhau, kasa kai?' ('How are you, brother?') and 'Ram Ram!' ('A respectful greeting') drifted through the air as villagers passed by. The cool air carried the scent of fresh earth.

After finishing their breakfast, the Kamat brothers thanked the Patil family for the delicious goodies. With the unsettling story still fresh in their minds, they decided to go for a stroll. The walk was an opportunity to discuss what they had just heard, to go through the details and make sense of it all. They needed to figure out what, if anything, they should do about it.

"Chatur, want to go out?" Tej called out to him, who had grown heavy after his breakfast and had settled in a cozy corner.

The moment he heard Tej, Chatur jumped out of his sitting position, grabbed his belt in his mouth, and raced out into the open. Rain or sun, Chatur always liked it outdoors! Sniffing at tires, chasing cats, and barking at every little moving insect he spotted was his favorite pastime.

The Kamat brothers and Chatur stepped out of the main gate. A block away from Tanmay's house, Vicky kicked off the conversation. "Tanmay wasn't very convincing," he said. "What do you think? Why would this boatman suddenly appear after so many years? Where was he all this while?"

"The haunting might have been happening for decades, so maybe they didn't notice him until much later. But one thing is certain—he's around, and we need to find out why!" Tej said. "The villagers claim they've seen Anna, and we can't ignore the case of the missing tourists!"

"Maybe those tourists had an encounter with Anna, got so scared that they had a heart attack, or ran off, never to return!" Vicky said. "Or maybe they had an accident or fell prey to wild animals. It's all jungle beyond the waterfall! Anything's possible."

"Yes," Tej said. "There are several possibilities. Their disappearance may have a link to the haunting, or it may be a complete mutually exclusive incident."

"Should we talk to some villagers? Let's see what they say," Vicky asked. "Maybe they can tell us something more."

"Not right now!" Tej replied firmly. "If we start asking around, people will suspect we're here to investigate something. Tanmay's father will find out soon enough and might step in to cut short our vacation. Didn't you notice how he wanted us to stay clear of this ghost business?"

Vicky nodded; having understood Tej's point. "And you know what? People have this inherent tendency to go along with whatever others say or believe in. Some might have genuinely spotted Anna, while others may cook up stories around his sighting," he added. "We may never get the true picture."

"Yes, let's not rush. Let's observe first and see if we can find any leads. I'm sure we'll uncover something," Tej said. "What we heard yesterday was horrifying. While I don't dismiss the idea of paranormal activity, my logical, scientific mind still struggles to accept it."

As they walked a block further down the street, with their minds full of questions and several possibilities, they noticed a medium-sized truck approaching them. It was fully loaded with red bricks.

"There must be some construction going on nearby," Vicky remarked as the heavily laden truck passed by slowly, making a loud rumbling sound.

They walked another few meters with Chatur sniffing around in the bushes, when Tanmay's voice called out to them from behind.

"Vicky! Tej!"

As they turned, they could see him on a bicycle racing towards them. A minute later, he caught up with them and hit the brakes.

"Hey, guys! How about a trip to the Ganesha Temple? The sun isn't out yet, and the weather is nice and cool. If we start now, we'll be back in time for lunch!" said Tanmay, panting from the rapid cycling.

"That's great!" Tej said. They turned and started walking towards Tanmay's house. He got down from his bicycle to walk alongside them, holding its handlebar on the other side.

Chatur simply refused to head back. He tugged at the leash and looked at them with a whine, his eyes pleading for them to continue. "What kind of walk is this? We should have gone further! I was just about to smell the fresh tires of that car over there!" he thought.

Vicky tightened his belt to make sure he followed them. "Chatur! Don't be stubborn! We will be late! Didn't you hear Tanmay? We must be back before lunch!" he said.

Chatur had no choice but to obey. With a reluctant glance, he listened to Vicky and quietly trailed behind them.

It was Tej's turn to bring out their Mahindra Thar. Tanmay and Vicky got into the jeep with Tej at the wheels, and Chatur jumped in as well! He was not in his best mood. His walk was not complete!

The uphill drive to the temple was quite pleasant. As the jeep climbed the hill, the village below grew smaller and smaller, becoming a picturesque view in the distance.

As they reached the temple, they were greeted by a strong, cool breeze. Chatur loved it. He darted around barking in excitement! He was enjoying it thoroughly! "The decision to cut short the morning walk had paid off!" he said to himself.

Tej went to the edge of the cliff, took a deep breath, and exclaimed in delight, "Wow! Picture perfect!" They could get a view of the entire village and the lake as well.

The village houses appeared small. "It's like a Lego toy village set from here, isn't it?" Vicky said. Tej looked back at him and nodded with a smile.

The weather was clear. They could see the far end of the lake and part of the waterfall flowing downstream into the thick forest.

They turned and walked towards the temple. It was majestic. All white marble! Even more beautiful than what it appeared from down below. The villagers had made quite an effort to flatten the surrounding land to accommodate space for a large vehicle parking area and had put pavers all around the temple.

"Many plays organized by the villagers and Jatras (a fair coupled with some religious events) happen here," Tanmay said as he pointed to the neatly paved space behind the temple. "People from neighboring villages also visit during those events."

Tej and Vicky were surprised to see some people already out there early in the morning to sell flowers, coconuts, and Agarbattis (incense sticks) for visitors to purchase so that they could offer them to Lord Ganesha.

Tej bought some flowers, and they all entered the temple to seek the Almighty's blessings.

After Ganesha darshan, the Kamat brothers spent some time observing every detail of the temple's interior.

The Pujari was more than happy to show them around. He appeared to be about thirty-plus years old, fit, and tall, a personality that didn't match that of a Hindu priest.

"How long are you serving at this temple?" Vicky asked.

"Well, this is part-time for me. My father and all my forefathers were priests, and he used to look after the temple. But now that he's quite old and no longer fit to continue his duties, I've inherited this responsibility from him. Those who were in this profession have either moved on to seek better opportunities or left the profession altogether. There's no money in it!"

"I run a small cafe down in the village and serve Lord Ganesh part-time expecting nothing in return. I am here in the morning, at noon, and for the evening puja. Since my staff help in running the cafe, I don't need to be there all the time," he said with a smile.

"By the way, my name is Vivek; you can call me that!" he added.

"Nice meeting you, Vivek!" Tej and Vicky responded shaking his hands with a smile.

Once they were outside the temple, Tej rushed to their jeep and, in no time, pulled out a professional camera with a zoom lens and started clicking pictures of everything around.

He was a photography buff and didn't want to miss out on the beautiful surroundings and the view of the village and the lake from the top of the hill.

This was followed by a selfie session. Vivek joined them in some. It was almost lunchtime. The Kamat brothers and Tanmay decided to head back home.

They thanked Vivek for his hospitality and for showing them around and hopped into the jeep.

During the downhill journey, Vicky, driven by curiosity, asked Tanmay, "This morning, we noticed a truck transporting bricks. Is there any construction going on nearby?"

Tanmay said, "That truck belongs to Mr. Pedro. He owns a brick kiln, more of a small-scale brick manufacturing facility, on the outskirts of the village. He transports the bricks to the railway station by truck to supply to various faraway customers by train."

"He is a very good guy and donates generously towards all good initiatives taking place in the village. He is doing good business. He has built a massive, luxurious house near his factory and owns multiple luxury cars! I will introduce you to him someday," he added.

Post lunch, the Kamat brothers decided to unwind in their room for the rest of the day. Tanmay walked in with a servant with some mouth freshener. Vicky was the first one to grab a few servings.

Tej helped himself to a spoonful and said, "Tanmay, you know us. We are the adventurous outdoor types. The temple area is breathtaking. Is there a secluded spot where we could setup camp to get a good view of the village and the lake?"

"We should avoid setting up our camp near the temple. It would be inappropriate and could obstruct the devotees who are visiting," Vicky added.

Tanmay said, "You have hardly been here, guys! Are you bored already? Was there any shortfall in my hospitality?"

Tej said, "Oh, come on! It's nothing like that! You and your parents have been great—you've treated us just like family! It's just for a few days!"

Tanmay paused, thinking for a moment. After a brief silence, he nodded slowly and said, "Well, if you insist... I suppose I can't stop you. I agree, though—the temple area isn't suitable for camping. Quite a few people visit, especially in the evenings."

He paused, thought for a while and said, "I think I know a place just right for your camping. I just remembered—the hill is also known as Leopard Hill, so we must stay alert. Although we have not spotted any leopards on the village side in the last few years, we still shouldn't take any chances."

They informed Tanmay's parents about their plan. His father was perfectly fine but quick to warn them, "Do whatever you want, but don't go near the lake at night!"

"Baba, don't worry, we are camping on the hill, next to the temple. That's nowhere near the lake!" Tanmay assured him.

Tanmay's father seemed relieved. "Okay! Enjoy!" he said with a smile. "And don't forget to take some warm clothes along with you. It gets chilly out there at night."

Back in their room, Tej and Vicky quickly connected their camera to their MacBook Pro to download all that they had clicked on that day.

They opened multiple pictures and videos that were captured from the hilltop.

The lake was broader on the village side and tapered on the far side. It was huge, over a kilometer from the near side to the waterfall.

"Isn't the lake almost like the map of Sri Lanka? Like an emerald!" Vicky exclaimed. "Broader on the village side and tapering as it stretches to the far end."

"Yeah!" Tej replied. "The water is crystal clear blue in color! But if it were green, it would look like an enormous emerald from the hilltop!"

On the left side of the lake, there were signs of a small river gushing out of a small cave-like opening and joining the lake as the water over there was quite turbulent. It appeared that the lake was fed by this small river.

A few meters further away, the river and the lake joined a medium-sized waterfall that flowed into the adjoining thick jungle.

"What a beautiful water body! It's so perfect. like an AI-generated image! It doesn't seem haunted at all!" Vicky exclaimed.

5

The Night Watch

The next morning, Vicky, Tej, and Tanmay were all set for their camping adventure! They had packed all their camping gear, along with other essential outdoor equipment, neatly in the boot of their Mahindra Thar, while the tent roll was securely tied to the roof rack of the jeep.

After breakfast, they began their journey back up the hill, along with Chatur in the back seat. Just as they were about to reach the temple, Tanmay directed Tej to take a left turn onto a narrow side road.

The road was dusty, a mud track rather than a tarred path… it didn't seem like it had been used in a long time. The jeep wobbled as it bumped over the uneven surface, kicking up a puff of dust.

But seconds later, they reached a clean, spacious area—perfect for setting up a large tent and a cozy bonfire. It appeared untouched, as if few knew about it, with no trash or signs of prior use. Soft, thick grass blanketed almost the entire surface, making it an ideal spot for a picnic.

"Hardly anyone knows about this place," Tanmay remarked. "I used to cycle up here with my friends to play cricket when I was a kid. To us, it felt like the Wankhede Stadium back then. Spaces do seem bigger when you're young, don't they? It should serve our camping needs well."

The entire village, an uninterrupted view of the glimmering lakebed, and glimpses of the waterfall were clearly visible in the distance. Beyond the waterfall, they could see its flow disappearing into the dense jungle. The 'Lake View Inn' and the boats at the jetty beside it looked tiny, like the tokens used in a game of Monopoly.

"Just what we were looking for!" Vicky exclaimed. "You've brought us to the perfect spot!"

Tej and Vicky turned toward the jeep and got to work without wasting any time.

Tanmay helped them lower the tent down from the top of the jeep. Setting it up was almost a plug-and-play effort for the Kamat brothers. The entire process was etched in their minds, having done it countless times before. From unfolding the canvas to securing the poles, every step came naturally to them.

A large tent good enough for five was up and ready in no time. It was a Wildcraft make, a brand famous for camping gear—sturdy enough to withstand strong winds, extreme cold, or heavy rain!

Thick, water-vapor-bearing clouds were gathering over the lake.

"We are going to experience some good rain tonight. Our ghost-spotting exercise is about to get even more exciting!" Vicky exclaimed. Tej responded with a smile of agreement.

"Ghost spotting! Is that why you came up with this camping idea?" Tanmay reacted, his eyes widening in surprise, his voice a mix of disbelief and nervousness.

"Well yes! Let's see what we find!" Tej said with a grin. "Your father told us not to go near the lake, right? We are following his orders! Aren't we?"

Tanmay continued to look worried.

"Don't worry, buddy! Anna can't see you from that far," Vicky chuckled. "You are safe out here. And you are not alone, are you?" he was trying to put Tanmay at ease.

Tanmay heard him out and nodded, but Vicky's assurance was of little help. He was tense as ever. He didn't like their idea at all.

Tej went inside the tent, set up a high-powered telescopic lens on a tripod, and focused it on the far side of the lake. He connected the lens to his professional digital camera and paired it with his MacBook, which he placed on a small table. The setup was designed so that whatever the lens captured could be recorded at the press of a button, with no further manual intervention, and displayed directly on the MacBook in real-time. The equipment was top-class, capable of capturing high-resolution videos from several kilometers away, and the high-capacity camera could record in sharp detail for extended hours.

The Kamat brothers ensured that the tent and surrounding areas were well lit with bright solar lanterns to keep wild animals away. They didn't want any leopards for company!

"These lanterns work for ten hours with one single charge and are self-replenishing, if the sun is kind enough," Vicky informed Tanmay. "Else we have to make sure they get a periodic recharge and would need an electric point."

"We can take them back home for charging during the day," replied Tanmay, visibly nervous, as he turned and hurried toward the tent.

Seeing Tanmay move away from them, "How do we make him comfortable?" Vicky whispered to Tej. "He doesn't seem to like the camping idea at all!"

"Well, Let's see how it goes," Tej said. "I hope he will settle down with time. If he doesn't, he can always choose to stay at home."

The team had packed enough food and drink for the night. Tej and Vicky lit a bonfire to keep things warm. But as it started getting dark, they decided to go back into the tent and start monitoring the far side of the lake and hit the record button.

Just as they entered the tent, Chatur, who was still outside, started growling. He was staring at some thick bushes, a few meters away!

Tej unlocked his fully loaded Glock 19 semi-automatic pistol, and Vicky picked up his Kukri (A traditional, curved knife from Nepal, used as both a weapon and a tool). Both darted towards the bushes. Tanmay followed them.

As they ran towards the bushes, they could hear rustling leaves. Whoever, human or animal, had already escaped before they could reach the spot!

Tej searched around a little and hunted for some clues. Tanmay joined him.

After a while, he pointed to a shoe lying near the bush. They were sure that the shoe was not around when they were setting up the campsite.

"Well, this leopard wears shoes! They're avid runners and athletes, aren't they? They certainly need these!" Vicky remarked with a sarcastic grin.

The Kamat brothers picked up the shoe and had a good look at it before placing it carefully in an evidence bag.

"The one hiding behind the bushes was clearly not a wild animal. Someone is taking note of our movements!" Tej said and looked at Tanmay. "We need to be watchful!"

Tanmay reached over and took the knife from Vicky, examining it closely. "Interesting knife, I must say. I've never seen anything like it before. It's quite heavy, and the handle is beautifully carved—clearly handcrafted! Where did you get it?" he remarked.

"Yeah! It's a Kukri. A junior gifted it to our father when he was in the Gorkha regiment of the Border Security Force. He let us keep it! In the right hands, it can be a lethal weapon, especially when combined with proper martial arts techniques. Gorkha soldiers carry it as part of their standard gear." Vicky demonstrated a few moves as he spoke, his hands slicing through the air, illustrating the precision and fluidity of each step.

Tej shook his head and teased, "Show off!" as Vicky demonstrated his moves, while Tanmay watched in sheer admiration.

Soon, the martial arts demonstration came to an end. The Kamat brothers made their way into the tent to begin their monitoring. The martial arts display had momentarily distracted Tanmay from thoughts of Anna, but the tension quickly returned. He fell back into his original mindset, as tense as ever, and followed the Kamat brothers inside.

Despite the threatening clouds above, all they felt was a chilly drizzle carried by the wind.

The Kamat brothers took turns to monitor the MacBook screen while sipping hot coffee prepared by Tanmay's mother.

"This coffee is a lifesaver!" Tej said with a grateful smile as he took another sip from his cup.

"We have plenty. I have more in another thermos flask for all of us!" Tanmay assured them.

They lost some time because of the intruder and missed the live feed of the real-time action on the MacBook. However, they weren't too concerned, as everything was being recorded automatically.

For the next few hours, they were glued to the computer screen while Chatur chose to be on guard to sniff out any further intrusion.

Time went by. "Absolutely nothing!" Vicky shouted, his voice dripping with disgust. "Did someone inform the headless boatman that we're watching? Why isn't he showing up? It's already an hour past midnight, and still nothing!" he added.

Soon it started pouring. Chatur ran inside the tent. They waited for another couple of hours, taking turns to glance at the MacBook screen.

Their luck was running out; all they could see was a nearly still, zoomed-in image of the far side of the lake.

"Let's catch the boatman another day," Vicky said, visibly dejected. Exhausted from the day's activities, they finally gave up and decided to take a nap.

The only one awake on night duty was Chatur, who had his eyes and ears alert and his keen, sensitive nose to sniff out anything out of the ordinary.

As and when rain eased, he took the opportunity to make occasional rounds of the camp area, and the camera continued to record every second captured by the powerful lenses that focused on the far side of the lake.

6
At the Brick Factory

The Kamat brothers woke up to a bright and sunny morning. The rainy clouds were nowhere to be seen. They had gulped down all the coffee brought by Tanmay during their watch the previous night.

As they stepped out of the tent, they saw Vivek, the part-time pujari of the Ganesha temple, approaching them with a large flask, a tiffin, and a few coffee mugs in hand, wearing a wide smile that stretched from ear to ear.

"I had noticed that you camped here last night," he said. "I thought of getting you some light breakfast. It's coffee and toast!" He then began pouring coffee into the mugs.

"Nothing like fresh coffee in the morning," the Kamat brothers and Tanmay exclaimed with a huge grin on their faces. It was just what they wanted.

All the hard work on the previous day had made them extremely hungry. They pounced on the breakfast like hungry wolves. Chatur got his share too!

In no time, the breakfast was over. Not a crumb left behind!

"I think I should have brought more!" Vivek said.

"No, no, this is just fine! Thank you very much!" the Kamat brothers said.

Right after breakfast, they thanked Vivek once again for his hospitality, and a little later, they decided to head to Tanmay's home for a more substantial meal.

A cup of coffee and toast provided a good initial recharge, but everyone was eager to enjoy the delicious treats waiting for them at Tanmay's place.

They packed all the electronics and other belongings. Before leaving, they requested Vivek to keep a watch on the tent and to check if the solar lanterns needed a recharge.

"I certainly will, and I'll let my assistant know as well. He works here full-time. And don't worry about the lanterns; I'll make sure they're charged before nightfall. I have a room right behind the temple where I can charge them," he assured the Kamat brothers as he gathered his belongings.

Back at Tanmay's home, Tej ensured that all the electronics were recharged and ready for the night ahead.

Tanmay showed up in their room. "Guys, how about a visit to the brick factory? I called Pedro a minute ago. He is there at the factory today and is more than happy to show you around."

"Why not?" Vicky replied, glancing at Tej. Tej nodded in agreement, his response immediate and enthusiastic.

"It's done then! We leave right after lunch!" Tanmay confirmed and walked away.

Tej and Vicky decided to take a good nap before lunch as they were in for another long night at the camp.

Right after lunch, they didn't waste any more time. The factory visit had to finish quickly for them to be back at the camp on time to spend another night looking out for Anna! All hopped onto Tanmay's jeep and headed towards Pedro's brick factory.

The factory was situated far outside the village. After a twenty-minute drive, they spotted it in the distance. As they got closer, Pedro's grand white mansion came into view—a sprawling estate with a glimmering swimming pool, meticulously curated landscaping, and towering palm trees swaying in the breeze. The estate was enclosed by a sturdy concrete wall, with a large wrought-iron gate guarded by a couple of security personnel. Just beyond the entrance, three sleek luxury cars with polished exteriors gleaming under the sun were parked in perfect alignment, adding to the aura of wealth and sophistication as they drove past.

Moments later, the jeep came to a stop right in front of Pedro's brick factory. Tanmay reversed the vehicle and parked it on one side to make sure that it did not obstruct the entrance.

They saw Pedro walking toward them, with a welcoming smile lighting up his face. He was a short, stout, middle-aged man, had lost most of his hair, and wore a thick gold chain like those worn by West Indian fast bowlers. He had an expensive Ray Ban eye shade tucked into his shirt pocket and a branded smartphone in his hand, which looked expensive as well.

"This man has taste," Tej murmured as he got out of the jeep.

"Pedro is of the flamboyant type. He likes living life king-size and is very conscious of the brands he uses," Tanmay whispered back with a grin.

Pedro seemed to be very excited to see the Kamat brothers. "Well! Well!" he exclaimed. "All visitors want to spend their time by the lake, or at the temple, or in one of those cafes! You are the first ones who have asked for a tour of my factory! Welcome!"

As Pedro escorted them inside, a bulky, over six feet tall man approached them.

"James, my foreman or production manager. He handles the entire factory. He will show you around," Pedro said. "I will see you in my office once he is done." With that, he gave them a polite nod and walked away, leaving them with James.

Unlike Pedro, James appeared to be strict and grumpy, with hardly any smile on his face. He showed no emotions.

"This way, please!" James directed them in his rough and tough voice and led the Kamat brothers and Tanmay to the factory shed. Chatur quietly tiptoed behind them.

He appeared to be quite knowledgeable in brick making and explained each step in the process with utmost clarity. Most of the work was done manually, while some steps were handled by highly advanced, precision-engineered machines.

The Kamat brothers saw this as an opportunity to set aside their investigator avatar and wear their engineering hats. They were especially intrigued by the workings of the smart machines, surprised to find such a state-of-the-art setup in a small factory.

Once the factory tour was about to get over, "Quite interesting! You are an expert!" Tej said to James in appreciation, hoping for a smile in return.

James ignored him and silently led them to the finished goods store. Finished bricks were stacked up neatly. It appeared that they were ready for dispatch. Tej, out of curiosity, picked up a brick to take a close look at it.

No sooner he lifted the brick, James rushed towards him, snatching it from his hands. "You are not supposed to touch the material, sir!" he shouted, his voice so loud and sudden that it almost deafened Tej, leaving the air charged with tension.

Tej was shocked! He froze for a couple of seconds! He didn't expect James to become so rude, and that too for a silly reason.

"What's the big deal in taking a look at a brick?" he thought to himself as he glanced at Vicky.

Vicky's face showed surprise as well!

Seeing all this happening, Chatur growled, ready to pounce on James and grab his neck. He didn't tolerate any misbehavior towards his masters. Vicky was quick to hold his collar tightly and avoid any further trouble.

Pedro saw what was happening from a distance and rushed towards them to calm things down. "Please forgive James; he is very good at his work but rarely interacts with people outside the factory. He has been with me since he was a teenager, and this factory is his life! He doesn't like anyone touching anything here, me included," he requested the Kamat brothers in an apologetic tone.

They didn't take James's behavior to heart. Instead, they ended the episode by apologizing and ensuring he felt comfortable.

James appeared to calm down as he put the brick back in its place.

To prevent any further awkward incidents, Pedro decided to stay with his guests for the remainder of their visit.

As they exited the finished goods store, they noticed a small, neat warehouse in the distance, located within the compound of the brick factory. It seemed unrelated to the brickmaking business.

"What's that?" Vicky asked Pedro.

"That? That's the space I have provided for my nephew Andrew. He stores all his stuff over there. He is into adventure sports, mostly water sports, whitewater rafting, and things like that. He organizes adventure camps for tourists and conducts training and certification programs for serious water sports enthusiasts to take it up as a profession. He is hardly around. His training ground is somewhere else. The waterfall here is too narrow, steep, and dangerous for such a sport," Pedro said.

Both Tej and Vicky were very much into adventure sports and insisted on checking out the warehouse.

James called out to another guy, "Pravin! Pravin! Where are you?"

A skinny, short boy with curly hair in his late teens, who appeared to have a limp, hurried toward them. He wore simple cotton trousers and a soiled T-shirt, suggesting he had been doing some manual work earlier that morning.

"Pravin! What happened to your leg?" Tanmay inquired.

It was no surprise that Tanmay knew Pravin; in the small village of Ganeshpuri, everyone was familiar with one another.

Before Pravin could respond, James quickly stepped in. "Pravin twisted his ankle this morning while lifting the bricks."

Both Tej and Vicky had a good look at Pravin's foot. "A bad sprain indeed!" Vicky said.

"Pravin, can you bring the keys to the warehouse?" James ordered.

Pravin limped his way to Pedro's office and returned with a bunch of keys. He was quick to find the right one for the warehouse lock and opened it.

The warehouse had different equipment related to adventure sports. In one corner, several rafts were stacked over each other in a deflated condition. Other equipment, such as paddles, pulleys, and ropes, was neatly arranged. Tej and Vicky looked at all the equipment with a great interest, but it made no sense to Tanmay, who hoped to get out of the warehouse as soon as possible.

Vicky noticed a green-colored wall, often referred to as a 'gallery-wall', that had numerous photo frames. He glanced at all the neatly framed photos, and noticed young lad, presumably in his mid-twenties, appearing in almost all the photos.

Pointing to one of the photos he asked Pedro, "Is that your nephew?"

"Yes, that's Andrew! And most of these are photos of practical training sessions he conducts. He is a certified trainer!" Pedro said, beaming with pride.

"We are into adventure sports as well. Mind if we take some pictures?" Tej asked.

"Please go ahead," Pedro replied.

Tej pulled out his iPhone 15 Pro Max and aimed its camera at the wall. He clicked some of the photos. Some had Andrew in it, and some didn't.

As they stepped out of Andrew's warehouse and walked towards Pedro's office, Vicky pointed to a truck parked beside the finished goods store. A few workers were busy forklifting sets of bricks onto the truck, their movements efficient as they carefully stacked the heavy loads, ready for delivery. The sound of the forklifts echoed in the background as the workers coordinated seamlessly, moving swiftly to load the truck.

"That must be your truck that transports the bricks to the railway station. We saw one while we were strolling on the street next to Tanmay's house," he said.

"Yes," Pedro replied, guessing that Tanmay must have informed them already about his business. "In fact, I own two that work in shifts. Ganeshpuri station, you know, is more of a platform than a station. Trains only halt there twice a day—once at noon and again at night."

"You know how the train system operates—they're rarely on time. That's why you'll often find one of my trucks loaded with bricks, waiting to unload onto the next train that arrives. I run a small business that caters to the construction needs of small developers who build individual houses and standalone buildings. And it's all going well, by god's grace! But you can't rely on one business all your life, so recently, I've invested in other ventures as well!"

The tour ended. Pedro escorted them in his plush, air-conditioned cabin—a stark contrast to the bustling factory outside. Rich mahogany furniture, soft ambient lighting, and the faint aroma of leather filled the space. A large window framed a sweeping view of the serene landscape, enhancing the cabin's refined atmosphere. It felt less like part of an industrial workspace and more like the corner office of a top executive in a corporate firm.

A maid entered with a tray of tea and fresh, premium Nankhatai biscuits. These traditional Indian shortbread biscuits, made with flour, semolina, and ghee, had a rich, crumbly texture and a delicate, sweet flavor, instantly triggered Vicky's salivary glands, making his mouth water in anticipation.

The deep aroma of high-quality Darjeeling tea filled the space, blending with the scent of leather. She arranged the tea on the table, and Pedro invited them to join.

Soon, they were sipping the tea and nibbling on the delicious biscuits. As usual, Vicky made sure to clean up his plate, not leaving a crumb behind.

During tea, Pedro inquired about Vicky and Tej, learning that they were studying engineering and just a semester away from graduation.

As the conversation flowed, he reflected on his own past, mentioning that due to financial difficulties, he had been unable to pursue education beyond basic schooling. He stressed the importance of education, admitting that he had always regretted not being able to complete his graduation.

Sensing the sincerity in Pedro's words, Tej offered an encouraging thought. "There's still time. You can still join the finest universities and fulfill your dream of acquiring a degree through distance learning programs."

Pedro chuckled, shaking his head. "Well, I'm nearing my fifties now. I don't think I have the patience to hold a book again or sit for an exam," he said with a laugh.

The conversation soon drifted toward many other interesting topics—stories of Pedro's diversified ventures and the changing times in the village. Despite the difference in their ages and backgrounds, the discussion flowed effortlessly, filled with laughter, insights, and a shared appreciation for life's lessons.

At one point, Tej leaned forward and whispered, "Mr. Pedro, some people in the village have been talking about the headless boatman. Have you heard anything about it?"

Pedro raised an eyebrow before breaking into a chuckle. "Headless boatman? Well, that sounds like a good topic for a fiction book or an OTT series," he said, shaking his head in amusement. He let out a hearty laugh, clearly taking it as nothing more than a ridiculous rumor. "Whoever told you this must be watching a lot of horror movies! Next, they'll say ghosts are running the brick factory at night," he added with a smirk, dismissing the idea as pure superstition.

Time passed quickly, and soon it was time for Tanmay and the Kamat brothers to bid goodbye to Pedro. They thanked him for his time, shaking his hand warmly. "It was great to see the place," Tanmay said with a smile. "Thanks for showing us around."

Pedro returned the smile. "Anytime, glad you enjoyed it."

"We'll be on our way now," Tej added, nodding in appreciation.

Pedro gave a quick nod as they left. "See you around, and drop in for a chat when you want to. I travel a lot, so

Tanmay, make sure you call before deciding to meet," he said. "And yes, give my regards to your father."

With a final wave, they made their way toward the jeep, their conversation fading as they left the factory behind.

On the way home, they talked about Pedro. Tanmay shared more on his inspiring journey of rising from the son of a humble fisherman with only a basic primary education to becoming a successful entrepreneur.

The Kamat brothers were quite impressed. "He's very down-to-earth and approachable. It's clear that all his success hasn't gone to his head," Tej remarked.

"Tej, you know what? Pedro seemed to have never even heard of the headless boatman. With the whole village worried about his presence and prayers being held for protection, it's surprising that someone as involved in the village as Pedro would be completely unaware. And when you mentioned it, he just laughed it off and dismissed it altogether. Is he really that clueless, or is he hiding something?" Vicky asked, looking thoughtful.

Tanmay interjected, "I don't blame him. Mr. Pedro is a hard-working man and is mostly traveling. He has invested in several businesses and is hardly around. So, keeping track of everything happening in the village isn't easy for him. It's very difficult to get an appointment with him—we were quite lucky to catch hold of him today!"

"Hmm... even with the headless boatman being around for about four years now? That's hard to believe," Vicky replied, shaking his head.

Tej, who had been listening carefully, finally spoke. "Vicky, I was watching Mr. Pedro's expression the whole time I brought up the topic. And you know what? I didn't catch a single sign that hinted he was hiding something. But you have a point—maybe he's just a real good actor. Shrewd businessmen can be excellent actors too. Let's keep this at the back of our minds."

They reached home before five in the afternoon. "We have some time," Tej said and looked at Tanmay and Vicky. "Why don't we look at the recording that happened last night? We may get some leads." He started connecting the gadgets.

"Do you really think we will find something?" said Vicky. His voice was laced with doubt.

But Tej was hopeful. "Well, let's give it a try!" he said. "We have nothing to lose."

All the electronics were already charged up and ready for use. In minutes, Tej was all set to download the video.

It was a recording that lasted well over four hours, and even on the fully loaded MacBook, it took some good amount of time to download. As the Kamat brothers and Tanmay waited patiently, the progress bar inched forward at an agonizingly slow pace.

Tanmay appeared tense, his fingers drumming lightly on the table. The room was silent except for the faint hum of the laptop's fan and the occasional creak of a chair as someone shifted in place. Every now and then, one of them glanced at the screen, hoping for the download to finish sooner…

Finally, the progress bar reached 100%, and the download was complete!

"I will play the video in 2x fast forward mode and slow down if we find something," said Tej. "Otherwise, it will take us hours to go through it!" and clicked on the play button.

7
The Headless Boatman!

The Kamat brothers and Tanmay were glued to the MacBook screen, eagerly searching for any sign of activity.

The video display indicated that an hour had passed, but still, nothing appeared!

After another hour, there was still no sign of anything!

The camera had captured a near-still image with occasional appearances of Chatur, who was patrolling the camp area at night and happened to find himself in front of the lens on several occasions.

Another hour went by, still nothing!

"I think we can name the video 'Chatur's Night Out'," Vicky exclaimed, frustration evident in his voice.

"What a waste of time!" Tej muttered, his frustration clear. "Let's stop the video and head back to the tent."

Normally calm and collected, Tej's patience had worn thin as he reached for the trackpad to stop the video.

But just as his hand hovered over it, something caught his eye. He froze. "Wait—look at that!" His voice was sharp with surprise, a hint of unease creeping in.

Vicky and Tanmay, just as they were about to leave the room, turned back, walked to the study table, and focused their attention on the MacBook screen.

They could see fog creeping up from one end of the lake, near the spot where the river water gushed into the stillness. Then, slowly, a shape began to emerge from the mist—a boat, moving eerily from the cave where the water had surged out.

Anna!...

Looming at the boat's rear sat the headless boatman in a white gown. His huge frame, nearly seven feet tall, seemed to blend with the shadows. A flickering lantern cast an eerie light around him. Where his head should have been, there was only a jagged neck, oozing slow trickles of blood.

"No human being can be that large," Tej whispered, his tone slightly nervous.

"Who says he's human?" Tanmay replied, his voice trembling with fright and confusion.

The boat moved slowly toward the middle of the lake. After a while, it drifted dangerously close to the edge of the waterfall. By then, thick fog had engulfed it, making it barely visible! The Kamat brothers and Tanmay were in a state of shock, frozen in place as they stared in disbelief!

A few minutes later, the fog thickened, shrouding the boat until it completely vanished from sight!

Tej reached for the MacBook, his focus sharp as he checked the video. He skimmed through it frame by frame, desperate to find a glimpse of the boat—or its headless boatman.

With steady fingers, he zoomed in on some frames, his mind racing. Though a hint of unease gnawed at him, Tej remained calm and confident.

But there was nothing around except for the fog that gradually began to clear.

The room fell silent for a few minutes, creating an uneasy tension that hung in the air.

"So, Anna's ghost exists after all!" Vicky finally broke the silence, his voice barely above a whisper as he stared at his brother and Tanmay.

Tanmay was sweating profusely and appeared choked! He could hardly speak. He grabbed a chair nearest to him and sat on it.

Whatever he heard about Anna from the villagers all these years was undeniable proof now. He didn't dare to go near the MacBook screen to take a second look!

The Kamat brothers were unsettled as well, but they poured a glass of water for Tanmay, helping him to calm down.

After a long, tense silence, Vicky suddenly broke it, his voice sharp with disbelief. "What is all this? Some kind of Ramsay Brothers horror movie?" His attempt at humor had made the situation feel even more real—and even more terrifying.

"This is not a movie! It's real!" Tanmay muttered, his mind swirling with horror and confusion. The weight of what he had just experienced was almost too much to bear.

"I'm not going back to the camp!" he continued, his voice shaking with fear. "I-I've had enough of this! I should have never told you about Anna!" His words spilled out in a frantic rush, as if he made a terrible mistake.

Tej and Vicky were shaken, but they had started to regain control, their minds focused on handling the situation. The lingering tension, however, still hung in the air.

"Tanmay, I know this has been terrifying... but we need to take a step back. Let's give ourselves some time to process it and start fresh tomorrow, alright?" Tej said, his voice trying to sound reassuring, though he wasn't entirely sure he believed it himself.

But Tanmay wasn't listening. His eyes were wide with panic, and his breath still came in short, quick gasps. "You don't get it! He is out there! And he is real!"

Tej placed a hand on his shoulder, his voice gentle but firm. "Tanmay, we'll deal with this together, alright? But right now, we need to calm down. We'll figure things out, one step at a time."

Slowly, after a few tense moments, the room seemed to settle. The sharp edge of fear dulled, and the three of them were able to get back to their senses, though the weight of what had happened still hung heavily in the air.

"Yeah… Let's rest on it and figure out things in the morning," Vicky agreed.

Tanmay didn't utter a word. He didn't dare to step out of the room and decided to sleep in the guest room and have the Kamat brothers for company.

8

A Visit to Ganeshpuri Railway Station

The Kamat brothers woke up very early the next morning. Their busy subconscious mind could not let them sleep. Tanmay was still fast asleep on the coach next to their bed.

They made sure they didn't wake him up and quietly stepped out of the room. Chatur followed suit. He knew that it was time for his morning walk.

The sky was still dark with just a hint of light on the horizon. The air was cool and quiet, with only a few birds beginning to chirp. As they walked down the street, engrossed in analyzing last night's video, Chatur suddenly stopped, his ears pricking up before he turned and began barking loudly.

Tej shouted instantly, "What's up, Chatur?!" Seconds later, as they turned to see what had caught Chatur's attention, they spotted a red Lamborghini darting toward them. Though it was still dark, the faint light was enough for them to recognize the make and color of the expensive car at once, its headlights cutting through the gloom.

A split second before impact, they all leaped into the nearby bushes, there was no time to warn each other. It was pure reflex that saved them; a millisecond later, and all three would have been crushed beneath the car's wheels.

Tej and Vicky suffered some bruises. Chatur, being the most agile one, escaped without a scratch.

Tej was infuriated! "What's going on? Is it another rich spoilt brat who has lost his mind or is someone desperate to kill us?" he said. "Did you notice the license number or the driver?"

"Nope, didn't get a chance!" Vicky moaned, wincing as he slowly helped himself to his feet.

Helping each other, they slowly managed to reach their Mahindra Thar and opened the first aid box. After applying some Betadine antiseptic liquid and taking painkillers, they slowly made their way to their room for a quick nap, knowing there was still time for breakfast.

Tanmay was still asleep on the couch. As they lay down on the bed, their minds started to race with thoughts of what had just happened.

"Whoever it was, he is not from the village. No one here is rich enough to own a super luxury car," said Tej.

"What about Pedro?" Vicky replied. "He is the only one in the village who could afford one!"

Tej, while in deep thought, said, "Why would Pedro want to harm us? And I didn't see any Lamborghini parked outside his house. Maybe it was not his car that tried to run us down!"

"No idea. It might not be him at all—maybe someone else is using his car or even stole it! Besides, there's a chance it wasn't parked outside his house when we visited his factory," Vicky said.

"But one thing is clear now: if this car was targeting us, then there is something beyond Anna that we need to look at! First, someone was watching us at the camp, and now someone is trying to kill us! It's evident that someone knows we're investigating and wants to stop us! And that cannot be Anna. Why would a ghost, busy scaring people, be driving a Lamborghini and come after us? These events are certainly not of the paranormal variety," he added.

The discussion made Tej pause for a moment. After a while, he said, "Yes, if the intent was to harm us, it makes things even more interesting! But we need to be certain." He glanced at Vicky, who had already fallen asleep.

Tej turned onto his back, starring at the ceiling. The thoughts racing in his mind didn't allow him to sleep.

He decided to stay awake, give some time for the painkillers to act, and continued thinking about the case.

After a good thirty minutes of rest, he nudged Vicky and whispered, "Vicky! Vicky! Wake up!"

Vicky jumped out of his bed! "What's the matter? Is Anna standing right outside the room?" he groaned. The pain had still not subsided completely.

"Quick! Let's pay a visit to the train station," Tej said as he started to wear his shoes. "Hurry up! We need to be back before Tanmay wakes up."

Without asking any questions, a sluggish Vicky followed suit, still half-asleep and unaware of what was happening. In the next few minutes, he joined Tej in their Mahindra Thar, with Chatur occupying his usual seat.

On reaching the train station, Tej quickly parked the jeep behind a bush. Vicky was back in his senses by then.

They could see one of Pedro's trucks loaded with bricks waiting for the next train to arrive.

"Start a conversation with the driver and loaders; offer them some tea while I check the bricks," he said.

"Bricks? Why?" Vicky replied, his puzzled mind unable to grasp the reason.

Tej was not paying attention; his focus was on the task at hand. He jumped out of the jeep and headed toward the truck, and Vicky, realizing Tej's intent, walked over to the driver and the two loaders idling alongside the truck.

Vicky was very good at making friends. He walked up to them, and in a few minutes, he pulled them into a conversation. Soon he was seen having tea and biscuits with the truck driver and the loaders at the only tea stall by the railway platform.

"That was fast!" Tej murmured to himself, a hint of admiration in his voice.

Without wasting any more time, he sneaked behind the tea stall, careful not to get noticed.

He jumped onto the truck and started to examine some of the bricks. In about ten minutes, he was done. He jumped out, returned to the jeep, and waited.

Vicky enjoyed tea and biscuits with the driver and the loaders, paid the tea stall owner, and joined Tej.

On their way back, Vicky asked, "What were you doing on the truck? Did you find anything interesting?"

"Nope, nothing unusual about these bricks. I just wanted to confirm something," Tej said. "James acted strangely when I picked up that brick, remember? I just wanted to see what was so special about them. Turns out, they're just like any ordinary bricks. Maybe James didn't have any hidden motives behind his behavior."

Even though Tej had an answer for Vicky, it was clear he wasn't convinced himself. There was still something on his mind as he fell deep into thought.

Vicky chose not to press him further. He was accustomed to Tej's odd behavior at times, but it always seemed to have a purpose in the end.

9

Observation Deck

By the time the Kamat brothers reached Tanmay's home, breakfast was being laid out. They sneaked back into their rooms without getting noticed and found Tanmay fast asleep.

They quietly took off their shoes, slipped into their slippers, and took turns using the attached washroom to freshen up.

The sound of running water filled the silence. By the time they were done, Tanmay had woken up and was slowly adjusting to the light.

Soon they could smell the irresistible aroma of filter coffee, which dragged them to the dining table. A while later, they were munching on some Upma (a popular dish in the southern part of India) and sipping coffee.

Vicky didn't mind back-to-back breakfasts. He grabbed the largest plate he could find and ensured that it was filled to the brim!

Tanmay freshened up and joined them, he was lucky to find his share left in the bowl. He quickly helped himself, knowing that if he'd been a few minutes late, Vicky would have gobbled it all! He was aware of his endless craving for food!

Just then, Tanmay's mother entered the room, followed by a servant carrying another bowl of steaming upma, her face lit with a warm smile.

"She must have noticed Vicky's appetite by now!" Tej said to himself, grinning as he glanced at Vicky, who was already busy shoveling another generous spoonful into his mouth.

Tanmay's father joined them at the table with a smile. "How is camping going? I hope you are enjoying your stay," he inquired.

All nodded with a big smile.

"You're not venturing to the far side, are you? Tanmay, their safety is your responsibility!" he doublechecked with Tanmay as he helped himself to some black coffee.

"No, we have not been to the lake! Vicky and Tej are enjoying the camping on top of the hill. We will be out there for a few more days," he assured his father.

Vicky and Tej nodded with a smile.

Chatur munching at his pedigree provided his feedback that he was enjoying the camping as well with affirmative howls. It appeared as if he was talking to Tanmay's father.

He looked at the dog and smiled with admiration. "Smart! I have never seen a dog like him before. Chatur means clever, isn't it? The name suits him!" he said.

As he raised his cup for another sip of black coffee, his eyes caught the bruises and Betadine stains on the Kamat brothers' arms.

"What happened?" he asked, a note of concern edging his voice.

"Oh, nothing! We just tripped and fell in a bush while we were playing with Chatur," Tej said.

"Please be careful next time!" Tanmay's father said as he served himself with some upma. "If you need a visit to the primary health center, Tukya can take you there. Our village might be small, but, let me assure you, we have the finest healthcare facilities and efficient doctors here."

"No need to worry; they're just minor bruises. We're fine!" the Kamat brothers replied, smiling reassuringly. "Thanks for your concern."

Tej and Vicky were relieved to see that Tanmay had settled down after the events of the previous day. He wasn't acting like a blabbermouth in front of his parents or the other servants in the house, despite what he had seen in the video. They remembered him from school as someone who couldn't keep anything to himself.

After breakfast, it was time for the Kamat sleuths to get to work. They called Tanmay into their room and shut the door behind him.

Anna's disturbing video from the previous night had left them rattled. But as investigators, they were quick to shake off their initial fear. It didn't take long for their natural curiosity and sense of purpose to kick in. With their minds focused on the task ahead, they were ready to dive into planning their next steps.

"Tanmay, we have decided to conduct a thorough investigation of this haunting. We won't leave Ganeshpuri until we uncover the truth!" Tej stated firmly. "Are you with us? If not, we'll move forward on our own."

Tanmay hesitated, his eyes darting between Tej and Vicky. His voice wavered slightly as he spoke. "Frankly, I'm not comfortable with this… and I'm not sure we should go any further with this Anna situation. Didn't you see the video? It… it looked like something out of a nightmare. Aren't you even a little scared? What if… what if we end up in danger? I just don't want to risk losing our life over this."

Tej took a moment and said, "Tanmay, you can opt out. There is no pressure for you to be part of this. See, we are used to such situations, and you are not. It's not in our DNA to leave any mystery unresolved. I know we have not dealt with a ghost before this. But there is always a first time!"

Tanmay paused, clearly unsure, as he struggled to find the right words. "You guys are really putting me in a tough spot here," he said, his voice filled with hesitation. "You're my best friends, and I can't just say no... but I honestly don't know what to do. What if everything goes wrong?"

Tej's expression softened, sensing his friend's fear. "Tanmay, if you decide to join us, we'll make sure you're safe. We won't put you directly in the line of danger—no risks. We'll handle the tough stuff."

They let Tanmay have a moment to think it over. As he mulled it over, Vicky suddenly spoke up, his tone firm and convincing. "But don't you think it's time we reached out to the far side? We need to get a better sense of the situation on the ground."

Tej nodded in agreement.

On hearing this, Tanmay panicked and paced around the room. "Are we planning to explore the far side after what we saw in the video clip?" he yelled at them.

The Kamat brothers calmed him down and made him sit on the bed. Vicky sat next to Tanmay, wrapping an arm around his shoulder to comfort him. "Tanmay, we must venture to the far side of the lake; we have no other choice! Just sitting in our tent on the hill and watching the 'boatman show' isn't enough. But did you hear what Tej said? Don't worry; we won't be taking you with us. The operation is dangerous, and we have no idea what we might face out there. Who knows, maybe Anna's ghost is real?"

"Maybe?" Tanmay replied. "After everything you saw in the video? This is real, guys! Anna will not spare us!"

"Look, Tanmay," Tej said. "We can't jump to conclusions without solid proof. And for that, we must go to the far side of the lake. Our decision is not going to change."

"We are the ones who are risking our lives. We have dealt with life-threatening situations before, and you have not. We can survive in the jungle for days, swim long distances, and manage to stay underwater using a snorkel for hours. We are professionally trained for all this! I can understand your situation. You're the kind of kind-hearted, well-mannered person everyone admires. Dangerous work like this isn't meant for someone like you—it's just not your kind of thing! I'm not saying this to look down on you, Tanmay. I truly respect who you are; I just don't want you to be put in harm's way because of something you're neither prepared nor trained for."

Tanmay stood there, absorbing their words, a sense of unease settling over him. He wasn't sure whether to feel relieved or more anxious. On one hand, he was terrified of what they were getting into; on the other, he didn't want to be left out, sitting on the sidelines while his friends faced danger. The thought of being left behind bothered him.

After a long silence, he shifted uncomfortably and asked, his voice quieter but laced with uncertainty, "I get it... but if I'm not supposed to do the risky stuff, then where do I fit in? What can I do to help?" There was a vulnerability in his question, a mix of fear and the desire to contribute.

Tej paused for a moment, thinking, before responding. "How about this: you can manage the 'Observation Deck' at the camp and keep an eye on the lake area. Stay in constant touch with us while we explore the far side. Use a satellite phone to alert us to any potential dangers and call for help if things get out of hand."

He smiled reassuringly. "That way, you'll still play a crucial role, and you'll be safe from Anna and his wrath!"

Tanmay's timid heart began to skip a beat again. He said, "Look guys, I would rather be with you even at the far side of the lake than alone in the tent with that spooky Anna out there! I can't imagine me being out of my house alone at night from now on."

Seeing his friend's hesitation, Tej thought for a moment, then added, "Alright, how about this—let's find someone to keep you company. You won't be alone, and we'll make sure you're in a safe spot while we handle the rest. How does that sound?"

Tanmay looked up at him, his expression softening slightly. After a brief pause, he nodded, appearing more at ease with the new plan. "Yeah, that sounds better. I can do that."

Tej and Vicky were aware of how important an 'Observation Deck' was in such operations. They needed to find someone they could trust and who Tanmay would be comfortable with, and that too very quickly.

After a few minutes of silence, Vicky finally suggested, "How about Tukya? Are you comfortable with him?" Tej turned and looked at Tanmay for a response.

To him, it didn't seem to be a bad option at all. "He is like an elder brother to me, very strong and brave. I will feel much safer with him around! With his support, maybe yes," Tanmay agreed.

"Hmm, okay," Tej thought for a while and continued. "Tukya is a good choice. He seems like someone with a sensible head over his shoulders. He can join our team. But I have one concern: He is very close and loyal to your Baba! What is the guarantee that he won't share our plan with him? The moment your Baba finds out, won't he put an end to our investigation?"

"Leave that to me! Tukya will not do anything that will put me in a spot. I am certain that he will be more than happy to join and support us," Tanmay assured.

The Kamat brothers were relieved to hear this. Vicky said, "Okay! Tanmay, it's your responsibility to make sure that Tukya maintains secrecy on what happens from here on."

Tanmay nodded in agreement. "Let me call him," he said before rushing out of the room.

Moments later, he returned with Tukya, who took a seat beside him.

The Kamat Brothers appraised Tukya on their findings and outlined their plan.

"Not a word should go out to anyone in the house or to my parents!" Tanmay cautioned him. "Whatever we do or learn should remain within us."

"Ever since Anna returned, the village hasn't been the same. It's dead after seven p.m. I'm eager to be part of the team and help unravel the truth. I'll do anything within my capacity to prove my worth," Tukya replied. He was sharp and didn't need much explanation or convincing.

Tej and Vicky then turned toward their MacBook and pulled up Google Maps. They spent some time checking different routes. Tanmay and Tukya watched, their faces puzzled—they had no idea what they were doing. Once they were done, they walked out of the room.

Tanmay reminded his father once again about their decision to continue camping at the temple hill but didn't share the reason behind it. "Tukya is also joining us," he added.

"Tanmay, good that you are taking Tukya with you; I am less tense now. I want you and your friends to have the best time together! Just don't venture into the far side of the lake! That's my only request," he reiterated.

"No! Baba, you're worrying unnecessarily. You don't need to check with us repeatedly. We're camping on the temple hill, right? And that's nowhere near the lake!" Tanmay assured him.

Vilasrao Patil was relieved to hear this. "Ah, yes! You're right! I remember that now. Enjoy yourselves! It's just that I'm a bit overly obsessed with this Anna situation and want you and your friends to stay safe," he remarked, smiling as he walked away.

It was nearing five in the evening. The gang hopped onto the Mahindra Thar. Chatur was not happy with Tukya around. First Tanmay intruded into his back seat, and now with Tukya, there was hardly any space left. He barked and howled loudly in a complaining tone.

Tej and Vicky couldn't hold back their laughter! "Chatur! The camp is not too far away," they said. "Please adjust!"

Chatur looked at them and was quick to understand and allowed Tanmay and Tukya to occupy the back seats. As there was not much space left for him, they decided to accommodate the big and bulky bog on their lap with a big smile.

Time was running out. This whole episode of accommodating Chatur in the back seat took a while.

Once everyone was seated comfortably in the vehicle, Tej raced it on the well-tarred roads and then up the hill.

"Chatur is definitely quite strong and heavy!" Tanmay remarked, raising an eyebrow. "He doesn't seem that big when you see him from a distance."

Tej chuckled, nodding in agreement. "Yup, he's a big dog now! He's grown so fast, it's hard to believe sometimes. Time flies!"

In no time, they reached the camping spot. Tej parked the vehicle next to the tent, making sure it wasn't in the lens's line of sight. He wanted to keep the jeep within view to prevent any intruders from tampering with it or the equipment inside.

Vivek was waiting for them at the campsite after the evening puja, holding a coffee flask, a few mugs, and a basket filled with hot samosas—neatly wrapped in tissue paper! He had made sure there was enough for everyone, especially Vicky.

"Vivek! What a pleasant surprise! But how did you know we'd be arriving now?" Vicky asked, his eyes fixed on the basket. The aroma had already driven him crazy.

"Well, Tanmay called me around the time you left," Vivek replied, his usual cheerful smile in place.

"Vivek, thank you for doing all this for us! But we will not be able to enjoy these samosas while you just watch us eating. Today you should join as well," Tej requested.

They lit the campfire and enjoyed the coffee and samosas. Chatur ate two and asked for a third one!

"You are not getting another one! Do you want to fall sick? You are part of the mission, and you have a big role to play!" said Tej, shooting a stern look at Chatur.

Chatur realized there was no use in insisting. "No extra treat for me," he grumbled as he quietly walked away, sat next to Vicky, and noticed four samosas on his plate!

"Not fair! He's part of the mission too, isn't he?" Chatur muttered to himself, turning his head away in silent protest.

"Samosas from my cafe are the best in the village. People buy them as soon as they are hot off the wok! The moment I knew you were heading back here, I made sure that my chef made some extra, especially for us, and he did it in quick time!" Vivek remarked proudly as they relished another bite.

While they were enjoying the samosas, "What is Tukya doing here? And why are you recording the lake view?" Vivek inquired; his voice tinged with suspicion. "I saw a telescopic lens aimed at that area," he pointed to the far side of the lake as he spoke. "What are you guys looking for? The lake is beautiful during the day and at night when the moon is out, but there's nothing interesting to see after dark—especially tonight."

By this point, the Kamat brothers had developed a strong bond of trust with Vivek. It had become increasingly difficult to keep their mission a secret from him, and they felt it would be unfair to start feeding him a roundabout story.

Vicky exchanged a glance with Tej before turning to Vivek. "We need to know—can we trust you with this?" he asked, his tone serious but not unkind.

Vivek met his gaze without hesitation. "Of course. You've got my word," he said firmly, with a reassuring smile.

They briefed him about the evidence that they captured on camera and the fact that the headless boatman exists. They shared with him their plans of exploring the far side of the lake. Tej played the video captured on the camera for Vivek.

Vivek could hardly believe his eyes! "This is terrifying! Ganapati Bappa! Only you can save us!" he exclaimed, his voice trembling with shock and fear. "I can't believe this is real! Villagers here have a habit of churning out ghost stories. I hear those almost every evening at my café. It's a favorite pastime for villagers and a great source of entertainment for the tourists who love to hear such spooky tales. I have heard this boatman story as well. But now it appears this Anna's ghost is far from being a figment of someone's imagination!"

Although Vivek appeared shocked momentarily, he gathered all his courage and returned to normalcy in a few minutes. He was not chicken-hearted like Tanmay.

He paused for a moment, his expression thoughtful, before insisting, "Can I join you guys? I'm really interested in being a part of this. I can assist Tanmay and Tukya, if you think that's helpful."

The Kamat brothers exchanged a glance, weighing the offer. Tej nodded slowly, then turned to Tanmay and Tukya. "What do you think? Is this a good idea?"

Tanmay and Tukya looked at each other, then nodded in agreement.

Tanmay felt a sense of relief. With Anna's fear still in his mind, having one more person by his side at the camp made him feel much better.

"Yeah, we could definitely use the help," he said with a smile.

"Welcome to the 'Observation Deck'!" The Kamat brothers exclaimed.

"Okay! Great! Give me an hour, and I will race down and come back. I need to change my religious attire," said an excited Vivek.

"Sure, take your time," Vicky said.

Vivek quickly got on to his Enfield bullet and raced down the hill.

Soon they saw him back at the camp on his bike, in jeans and a t-shirt!

"That was quick! You didn't take much time!" Vicky remarked.

"We just didn't recognize you! You are in a completely different avatar! Fit like a sportsman who could easily try for a hero's role in a Bollywood film," Tej complimented Vivek as he made himself comfortable on a chair outside the tent.

"He is already playing his part in a real-life horror movie now," Vicky chuckled.

"Yes, I am indeed! We can call it 'The Wrath of the Headless Boatman'," Vivek laughed.

Tej chuckled along with him, but Tanmay wasn't in the mood. Although he was playing a part in the investigation, every time the topic of the boatman came up, it sent shivers up his spine.

"A movie... that's what they think this is," he muttered, a bitter edge to his voice. "When will they wake up and realize this is real—that we're putting our lives on the line?"

Everything was set perfectly once again. The telescopic lenses focused on the lake, the camera was all set to record, and the MacBook was paired and ready. Tej then pulled out a satellite phone, configured it quickly, and handed it over to Tanmay.

Next, the Kamat brothers gave a brief demonstration. "You can stay in touch with us using this satellite phone," Vicky explained. "If you need to alert us, call right away. Don't panic if you don't get an immediate response!"

"Listen carefully," Tej said, handing them a couple of emergency contact numbers. "There may be times when we're underwater, or the situation might not allow us to communicate. If that happens, we might turn off our headphones, so don't panic if you don't hear from us. And if you sense any danger, call these numbers immediately."

"Understood loud and clear. We're ready!" the team responded in unison, voices firm and confident.

The Kamat brothers pulled out a small box from their Mahindra Thar and handed over to them an additional pair of binoculars, a revolver, and a bullet case.

"Why these additional binoculars?" Tukya asked out of curiosity.

"Just in case you need to check any other area, use these instead," Tej instructed. "The telescopic lens must stay focused on the lake—nowhere else. We need to keep a constant watch for any impending danger. Remember, the camera's just a recording tool; it won't alert us to any danger on its own. One of you needs to keep constant watch while we're down there."

They also demonstrated to them how to operate the revolver. "It's loaded with six bullets, and more are in the case. It's for your protection. Use it if you must!" Tej said.

Tanmay accepted it with trembling hands, and the peace-loving, religious Vivek decided to stay away from it! But Tukya was familiar with weapons. "I am familiar with guns," he said confidently. "I have accompanied Patil Saheb on his hunting trips. Give it to me. I will handle it! I can shoot accurately if it comes to that." He took possession of the revolver.

"Great!" Tej said, "And one last and most important thing, guys! Whatever happens down there! Do not leave the camp! I repeat! DO NOT leave the camp! Your job is to monitor and ask for help if needed."

All acknowledged with a nod.

Next, the Kamat brothers retrieved a large container from their jeep and opened it. They pulled out sizable metal pieces and began assembling something as the team watched with keen interest. Soon they had two mountain bikes ready!

They then filled air into the tires using their portable compressor unit. Tej then packed everything they needed into a backpack, and both darted down the small, muddy road that served as a shortcut to the lake.

Chatur galloped behind them like a stallion. They had done a quick but thorough study of the terrain using Google Maps at Tanmay's home. The route was already etched in their minds. The team watched them with awe!

Once the Kamat brothers were out of sight, they walked back to the tent to start their monitoring activity.

Tej and Vicky reached the far side of the lake. They realized they couldn't use the bikes any further; the terrain ahead was too rocky and uneven.

"Hope we haven't missed anything," Tej whispered, as they hid their mountain bikes behind some bushes and started walking towards their destination with a mild-intensity torch to guide them. They didn't want to get noticed.

It was pitch dark and quiet. It was so dark, they could barely see a few meters ahead, with everything around them lost in the shadows.

The only sounds one could hear were those of thousands of crickets and a few frogs croaking at a distance. A cool breeze rustled the leaves, carrying with it a damp, earthy scent.

The Kamat brothers decided to take a brief pause and check the communication equipment. "Hello team, can you hear us?" Tej said in a low voice.

An excited Tanmay replied loudly, "Loud and clear, sir!" Tej's ears started ringing!

Tej whispered back, "Tanmay, can you please be a bit softer while speaking on the satellite phone? If you shout like this, I will be deaf before sunrise!"

"Very sorry, using this for the first time in my life. I will remember from here on!" Tanmay replied.

While Tej was talking to him, he noticed a bright torchlight in the distance. Someone was approaching them! Tej and Vicky switched off their torch and communication devices and quickly hid behind the bushes. Chatur followed suit.

When he was within a couple of meters, Tej and Vicky could see him clearly. They both couldn't believe their eyes!

"What is he doing here and that too at this hour?" They wondered and looked at each other astonishingly!

It was Mr. Vilasrao Patil, Tanmay's father!

"He was the last one on our suspect list," Tej murmured and looked at Vicky.

"What's he doing here? Did he think this was a good time and place for an evening stroll after dinner?" Vicky whispered, a grin spreading across his face.

Seconds later, Tanmay's father walked past them.

When Mr. Patil was at some distance away, Vicky whispered, "Let's keep what we saw to ourselves till we are one hundred percent sure of Mr. Patil's involvement. Let's not jump to conclusions. Also, no word about what we saw should fall on Tanmay's ears."

Tej nodded in agreement. "Good that we switched off the headsets," he whispered back. "Tanmay will not have any idea of what we spoke about!"

"Quick, let's see where he goes!" Tej signaled to Vicky that they should choose to swim by pointing to the lake. Any slight sound they made while walking would have alerted him.

Quickly stripping off their cotton clothes and tucking them away in the bushes, the two revealed their swimming trunks underneath. Grabbing their snorkeling gear from their backpacks, they swiftly put it on before slipping into the water and making an underwater dash to keep up with Mr. Patil.

The water was chilly, but the Kamat brothers were used to such temperatures.

Chatur quietly swam right behind them with his head high above the water. He didn't need any equipment. They got out of the water and hid behind a large rock on the banks of the lake.

From their hiding spot, they saw Mr. Vilasrao enter a small cave—the spot where the river met the lake.

"Exactly what we anticipated from the hilltop! There is a small river that feeds into the lake! Look at the turbulence!" Tej whispered to Vicky.

The cave was dimly lit, casting shadows on the walls. They could make out only Mr. Vilasrao and the shadow of one other person on the opposite wall. It seemed like he was speaking to him. Though their voices echoed in the silence, the words were unclear.

Vicky quickly pulled out his waterproof spy-cam and clicked some pictures in quick succession. He could capture Mr. Vilasrao clearly in the frame, his face sharp and unmistakable through the lens. However, when he tried to capture the other person, he just couldn't get a clear shot.

After a few minutes, Mr. Vilasrao walked back to the same path that led to the village. They waited patiently for Mr. Vilasrao to leave until he was completely out of sight.

Once he was gone, they exchanged quick glances and silently agreed to stay a little longer. Their focus now shifted to Anna, who had yet to make an appearance.

Hours passed, and still, no one showed up. The sky began to lighten, signaling that the sun would soon rise.

Tej suggested, "Let's setup the wireless camera and focus it on this path that leads to the cave. It has a good, long-lasting battery. It will capture whoever takes this road towards the cave, something our 'Observation Deck' will not be able to do from its current position."

They fixed the camera, and swam back to their bikes, dried themselves, wiped Chatur, and cycled back to the camp as it was almost sunrise!

Back at the camp, Tanmay, Vivek, and Tukya were eagerly waiting for them.

Tanmay appeared annoyed as he questioned the Kamat brothers, "Hey, I just couldn't speak to you! Why did you switch off your communications gear? I was tense!"

Tukya was quick to remind him, "Remember? They told us that they may not always be reachable!"

"We decided to stay underwater so that no one could notice us. We had to switch off our headsets!" Tej said.

"Did you find anything? Did you see the ghost?" Vivek inquired.

"No, not really," Vicky replied. "But we noticed a small river gushing out a narrow cave into the lake. The waterfall that you see from here begins, a few meters after the cave. And you know what? Someone had lit a lantern inside the cave; it's not deserted! There's definitely something going on in there!"

They kept the fact that they had spotted Mr. Patil near the cave to themselves as decided earlier.

"So, we've made some progress!" Vivek declared with a smile. "I'm heading home now and will return for my usual morning duties at the temple. Oh, and one more thing: my café will be the official 'food and beverage' sponsor for this mission from now on. Tanmay, please let your mother know—she doesn't need to go out of her way to prepare our meals anymore."

He further informed them, "If you guys want to take a shower or use the restroom, you can use my room, which is right behind the temple. Ask my assistant for extra towels and soap who stays there. He also has a room next to mine."

Tanmay assured the Kamat brothers that Vivek's Café is the go-to spot for tourists and villagers seeking authentic, healthy food, promising them plenty of tasty treats throughout their adventure. "Just one thing: it's going to be vegetarian. After all, it is a pujari's café!" he added, glancing at Vicky with a sly smile.

Tej was perfectly fine with vegetarian food; he nodded and smiled back at Tanmay with gratitude. Vicky, on the other hand, was not happy at all. He frowned and muttered to himself. "Veg-food! Yuk! I hope we wrap up this case quickly!"

"Tanmay, you can let your mother know that Vivek's café is supplying the food, but please don't reveal our mission to her!" Tej said.

"Yes, I know. Don't worry!" Tanmay replied.

He was visibly tired after staying up all night. "I'm heading home! See you guys in the evening!" he said, asking Vivek for a ride. Meanwhile, Tukya decided to stay back.

They bid goodbye to both and went for a shower at the restroom behind the temple.

As they returned, they saw a person walking towards them.

It was Vivek's assistant from his café, carrying a hamper and a couple of flasks. "It's breakfast time," he said, flashing a big smile.

They thanked him and pounced on the breakfast. The flasks were filled with hot masala chai (tea), and the hamper contained delicious veggie sandwiches. They relished the food before deciding to rest in the tent to recharge for another night at the far side of the lake.

It was about noon. They saw Vivek back with two huge thermally insulated food containers and another pack of mineral water bottles.

"Hey guys!" he said with a smile. "This should be good enough for today. But if you want anything else, just call my assistant. The guy who came in the morning? He will make sure food is delivered to your doorstep within thirty minutes. I am the local Zomato, Swiggy, here! There is no one else!"

"I'll bring Tanmay with me in the evening, so you won't have to pick him up," he added.

The Kamat brothers and Tukya thanked Vivek and grabbed their lunch packs. Chatur was served his share and settled into a corner of the tent.

10

Close Encounters

Three more days passed, clear skies and great weather! No sign of any big bad clouds. The Kamat brothers showed no indication of taking any action.

"Why have you suddenly relaxed? Have you given up?" Tanmay asked, pretending to be eager to take the case forward. Deep down, he hoped they would stop chasing after the spooky Anna.

"We have no choice, Tanmay. We have to wait!" Tej said. "Did you notice? It barely rained last time we went down there—just some light drizzle off and on. And did we spot Anna? No, we didn't! We have to wait for the right conditions."

Vicky added, "Anna, for some reason, seems to love bad weather!"

"There's no point in going to the far side when the chances are slim. We might end up finding nothing. If we go there too often, especially in clear weather, there's a good chance we'll get noticed," Tej pointed out.

"But why does Anna only appear during bad weather? What could be the reason?" he wondered.

"Anna lost his life in the midst of a terrible storm, which is why he now chooses to haunt that atmosphere," Vicky guessed. "It seems he unleashes his wrath only when the skies darken, and heavy rain begins to pour."

The Kamat brothers tuned into the weather forecast on the built-in radio of their SUV every single day, anxious for any sign that could bring them closer to spotting Anna. It had become their daily routine, a small ritual that kept their hopes alive.

Then, the forecast for the next day came through: heavy rains, lightning, and thunder! It was exactly what they'd been waiting for—perfect conditions to find Anna.

The next morning, the team could see thick cloud buildup over the lake and beyond, just as per the weather bureau forecast!

"The Rain Gods are kind to us today!" Vicky exclaimed.

Vivek was pumped up. He looked at Tej and asked him in excitement, "So, are you finally going to confront the headless boatman tomorrow?"

"We certainly hope so!" Tej replied. "Yes, there is going to be bad weather! But that does not guarantee anything."

The team spent most of the time inside the tent, monitoring the lake area and relishing the goodies that arrived from Vivek's café waiting for nightfall. Time flew by, and before they knew it, it was six in the evening already.

The rain started pouring down from the skies with no intent to stop.

As it got darker, Tanmay, Vivek, and Tukya took control of the 'Observation Deck'. Chatur stayed back to attend to his guarding duties, and the Kamat brothers darted down the hill one more time on their mountain bikes.

They hid their bikes at their usual place, got into the water, swam very close to the cave, got out of the water, and hid behind the same enormous rock.

The rain had intensified, accompanied by flashes of lightning and booming thunder. Although it was just around seven, the surroundings had turned pitch black. Every now and then, the skies lit up, making everything visible for a couple of seconds every time lightning branched out up in the skies.

"Good that we are out of the water," Tej whispered to Vicky. He knew that if lightning struck the water, it could be fatal!

An hour passed by, but there was no activity! The entrance of the cave was dark. The lightning had stopped momentarily, and it was pitch-dark all around once again.

"Is it an off day today for the headless boatman? No one seems to be around. Do you remember if there is a government holiday today, Tej?" Vicky inquired in his usual jovial mood.

"This is no time for cheap jokes!" Tej whispered, who was in no mood for a lighter moment.

By now, the rain had grown even heavier, coming down in heavy bursts. Strong winds howled through the air, making the cold even worse. An hour passed, but the Kamat brothers stayed still, watching the dark cave in silence.

Then, just as they were starting to lose hope, something caught their eye. A faint light flickered from inside the cave, casting strange shadows on the water. The only sound was the distant rumble of thunder.

Moments later, a midsize boat slowly appeared from the cave, gliding through the rough water without a sound, as if it was floating on air! Perhaps the rain had drowned out the hum of its motor… or was it moving on its own?

At the rear of the boat sat the headless boatman, Anna, gripping a lantern in his massive hands. His towering frame was draped in a cloak fastened tightly at the neck—his head was missing! A thin streak of blood trickled down one side of his gaping neck, vanishing into the folds of his cloak.

Thick fog built up around the boat created an eerie haze area, making it partially visible!

This time, they were so close that the boat and the headless boatman were unmistakably clear. It was exactly what they had seen in the video earlier, but witnessing it in person, just a few feet away, was far more terrifying than they ever imagined.

They couldn't believe their eyes! They could hear their hearts pounding loudly in the silence, and no words came out… their minds numb with shock.

As they stood frozen, still watching till a voice crackled on their headphones, it was Tukya "Hey Guys! Are you seeing what we are seeing from here? Anna is out there! Are you okay?"

His voice snapped them back to their senses. "Yes! Yes!" They whispered back. "We can see him clearly. Just a few meters away! But let's not talk any further! He may notice us!"

Vicky pulled out the spy camera and started clicking pictures.

When the boat was a few feet away from the waterfall, the fog intensified further. They could hardly see it. Moments later, the lantern was switched off, and the boat came to a halt. The Kamat brothers heard some two to three distinct splashes as though something had fallen into the water.

As the entire activity happened on the other side of the boat that faced the waterfall, they couldn't see a thing! The boat then turned and made a quick dash to the cave, while the dense fog began to recede.

Thankfully, the lightning had stopped.

Tej gestured to Vicky, "Quick, let's check what they dropped in the water."

In no time they were swimming underwater and surfaced after a few minutes. "Nothing!" Tej exclaimed, gasping for breath at the same time.

"Well, whatever they dropped must have floated downstream since the waterfall starts just a few meters from here," Vicky pointed out.

"Maybe not! Maybe we are experiencing what Anna wants us to!" Tej replied, his voice barely a whisper. "Maybe it's just our minds playing tricks—part of the haunting. We think we saw something... or heard someone fall into the water. But what if nothing ever really happened?"

The eerie feeling hung heavy in the air, and they didn't feel it appropriate to stay there any longer. They swam hurriedly back to the shore before the lightning lit up the sky again, got onto their mountain bikes, and raced to the camp.

Vivek, Tukya, Tanmay, and Chatur rushed to Tej and Vicky as soon as they saw them approaching.

"Thank God you're back safe and sound! What happened down there?" they asked eagerly.

Tej looked at the team and said, "We witnessed everything from just a few meters away. The whole scene was terrifying! But as we waited to investigate further, we sensed something was off. Something isn't right, and I can't explain it all to you right now. There's much more to uncover!"

They stood next to the bonfire lit by the team, grabbing some fresh towels to dry off and ensure they warmed up, avoiding the risk of catching a cold.

11

The Cave

The Kamat brothers were greeted with light showers on the next morning.

Vicky's voice had a touch of concern as he spoke, "There's something strange about this entire boatman episode — I'm sure something fell from his boat, but no matter how hard we searched, we couldn't find anything. Whatever it is, it's hidden from us, for now. We won't know anything until we enter that cave and check."

"Yes, let's wait till dark and find out!" Tej said. "I hope there is no lightning tonight! We must swim some distance to get to the mouth of the cave! Any lightning can put our lives at risk."

"Yes, let's hope so," Tej replied. The rest were hearing every word that they were saying.

Time raced as usual, and before they could realize it, it was about seven in the evening. It had turned dark.

Thick clouds were looming in the skies, but the rain had not kicked off.

Vicky and Tej started on their bikes. This time too, Chatur didn't accompany them. He was assigned the task of guarding the 'Observation Deck' once again. Although he loved being with the Kamat brothers on every adventure, he accepted his task willingly. He was a true team player.

Once they reached the far side, they hid their bikes at the usual place and were ready with their swim trunks on and snorkeling equipment. Fortunately, it was only drizzling, with no signs of lightning or thunder. They waited until it got a bit darker and walked a bit towards the cave to minimize the swimming distance before entering the water.

At first, the swimming was effortless, but as they approached the cave, they experienced a strong current gushing out of its narrow mouth. It got stronger as they swam closer and pushed them back. They had to exert more effort to cut through it and move forward.

Soon they spotted a very large rock right outside the mouth of the cave where the water was relatively still and appeared to be shallow. They quickly swam across towards the rock, hid behind it, and peeped inside.

Although the mouth of the cave was relatively small, it was much larger on the inside. There was just one lantern hung onto a large hook hammered into a rock that illuminated the whole area.

The river water was flowing rapidly to meet the lake on one side. The riverbank on the other side was at a higher level. They could see a manmade jetty with a boat anchored beside it.

The boat was bigger than the ones they had seen at the village lake jetty. It had a driver's room and a cabin in front, with a seating area at the back.

"Anna's boat? Didn't we see the same boat yesterday?" Vicky whispered.

"Maybe!" Tej whispered back, "Can't say!"

Vicky was quick to pull out his spy cam and click some pictures in rapid succession.

They waited for a good thirty minutes. As there was no activity, they got out of the water, jumped onto the raised banks, and put on their night vision goggles, and switched off the lantern with the intent to explore the cave unnoticed.

As they approached the boat, they heard some voices. "Hey, what happened to the lantern? Go and check immediately!"

They could sense that there were some people out there! One of the voices was quite familiar, but they could not recall exactly who it was!

Tej and Vicky did not want to get noticed and avoid any confrontation then. They jumped back into the water. Swimming to the banks was relatively easy and effortless, as this time they were moving in the direction of the water current.

They reached the banks in quick time, got back on their bikes, and raced back to the camp.

"Bad luck," Tej said to Vicky. "We hoped to find more."

"Well, there is always another day!" Vicky replied.

Back at the camp, they did not disclose anything. They had decided to keep the boat discovery a secret until they found something more concrete!

By now Tanmay was getting impatient. "What's our role anyway? Should we sit and watch? On top of that, you guys don't call! You don't talk! You keep your communication gadgets switched off! Are we really required here?" he complained.

Vicky walked up to him and wrapped his arm around his shoulder and said, "Listen, you, Vivek, and Tukya have a big role to play. Right now, it might feel like you're unwanted, and we admit things are a bit boring for you, but believe me, we won't be able to win this without a fully operational 'Observation Deck'!"

For the next couple of days, the weather remained pleasant—clear skies, a gentle breeze, perfect for a picnic. Each night, the camera kept recording, its lens capturing whatever it could. Every morning, the Kamat brothers and their friends eagerly reviewed the footage, hoping for a breakthrough. But time and again, disappointment greeted them—nothing out of the ordinary.

The only option they had was to enjoy the delicacies from Vivek's café and wait—wait for bad weather!

12

Beyond the Waterfall

The next day was a bright and sunny one. Soon after breakfast, Tej and Vicky decided to go for a stroll near the temple area and do some brainstorming in private. Chatur joined them.

"We must visit the cave again. This time, we might actually find something!" Vicky said, his voice filled with anticipation.

"Wait! Hold on!" Tej interrupted, his eyes widening with realization. "I think we've already found something valuable."

For a moment, he stood in stunned silence as the thought sank in. Then, without another word, they raced back to the tent.

Tej grabbed their MacBook and downloaded the pictures they had captured. He compared the boat they found in the cave with the one the boatman was using.

"It's identical! The same boat! Same color, same structure, same size!" Tej exclaimed, his voice full of disbelief. "And look at that huge scratch on the hull! It's the same!"

"Yeah, two boats can look identical, but that scratch—it's too distinct to ignore. That seals it—it's the same boat!" Vicky exclaimed, his excitement mounting. "Guess it's time to go in there again!"

"We still have no idea if anything was dropped in the water at all. Maybe we should check out the area at the base of the waterfall!" Tej suggested.

Vicky agreed, "Good idea! Let's do that instead. We'll for nightfall!"

They decided it was time to share their discovery with the rest of the team. Until now, they had intentionally kept the details about the boat they saw in the cave to themselves, not wanting to speculate without evidence.

Now certain that the boat in the cave was the same as the one used by the headless boatman, they gathered everyone and laid out the facts, the mystery still lingering in the air.

It was around nine at night. They picked up basic mountaineering equipment and started down the hill on their mountain bikes. Luckily, there was no rain in sight.

"No rain means a holiday for the boatman!" Vicky chuckled. "Less chances of us being spotted."

"Don't be so sure!" Tej replied, "We have to be careful."

Reaching the far side, the Kamat brothers swam to the edge of the cliff next to the waterfall, beyond the cave. Mostly underwater with their heads down, they breathed through their snorkels.

Finding a spot on the slippery rocks, hidden from view of the cave, they began setting up the rope for the descent. The rocks were dangerously slick. Though the drop was just over a hundred feet, a fall from this height onto those jagged edges could prove fatal.

They made sure the rope used for support was firmly secured to a large, sturdy rock and started climbing down. As the drop was not too much, they made quick progress.

Once they reached the bottom of the waterfall, Tej pulled out a powerful torch while Vicky ensured their Glock 19 semi-automatic pistol was unlocked. They braced themselves, prepared for any wild animal or unexpected danger.

At the foot of the waterfall, the shore was mostly flat, with smooth, slippery pebble stones beneath the surface of the cold water. The moon had turned the water silvery. It was perfect for another photo session, but the time wasn't right. They needed to investigate quickly and head back without delay.

The entire area was a dense jungle, filled with huge, thick trees, bushes, and shrubs. The air was thick with moisture, and the gentle rush of the waterfall filled the air. As they stood there, looking around, Vicky suddenly froze, his eyes narrowing.

"Hey! What's that?" he pointed towards the jungle and looked at Tej.

About twenty meters away, hidden behind some thick trees, he spotted a faint light flickering in the shadows. Both decided to walk towards it.

As they moved closer to it, a small wooden cabin came into view, its exterior illuminated by a dim, flickering forty-watt bulb hanging above a narrow patio. The area surrounding the cabin was cleared and well-maintained. It was evident that the cabin was not abandoned but actively used by someone!

They could see a thin mud road right next to the cabin, wide enough for one vehicle to pass, which led to somewhere out in the jungle.

"Why would someone live here? And where does this road lead to?" Tej whispered.

Vicky looked back at Tej and shrugged without an answer. They hid behind a bush for half an hour to watch for any movement around the cabin.

Tej said, "I will go inside. You give me cover. Do you have your semi-automatic unlocked?"

"Yes, all set!" Vicky said, quickly checking his weapon before confirming.

Tej tip-toed towards the cabin quietly. The cabin door had a manual lock. He quickly pulled out a toolbox from his backpack, worked on the lock to unlock it, and entered the cabin.

A few minutes later, he stepped out and made sure he locked the door again as he didn't want to raise any suspicion. He glanced around to check that no one was watching and joined Vicky.

"What did you find?" Vicky whispered.

"Let's get back to the camp first. I will tell you there," Tej replied.

Both climbed up the waterfall hill, the path steep and difficult. The rocks were slippery, and they had to carefully find footholds, gripping onto jagged edges to avoid slipping. The sound of the rushing water filled the air as they made their way to the top.

Upon reaching the top, they swam back to their usual spot. After catching their breath, they cycled back to camp.

13

All that Glitters is Gold!

𝓑ack at the camp, Tej quickly got off his bike and headed for the tent with a sense of urgency, not saying a word. The others followed him closely.

Vicky was certain that he had found something important. Leaning closer, he asked, "So, what did you find?"

All looked at Tej with curiosity and excitement.

Tej opened his backpack and pulled out a brick!

"A brick?" all exclaimed and looked at one another.

"What's the big deal about that? You guys went down the waterfall and came back with this?" Tanmay remarked, sounding unimpressed.

Tej glanced at Tanmay, his expression hinting that he was about to reveal something they could never have imagined.

Vicky explained to the rest of the team how they climbed down the waterfall to find the cabin a few meters away and the fact that it was used by someone.

Tej continued, "When I entered the cabin, I saw a lot of bricks neatly stacked on one side. Some were packed in waterproof plastic boxes, while others were left out in the open."

"Who packs bricks in plastic containers?" Tanmay said. He was listening to the Kamat brothers with undivided attention.

Tej grinned at Tanmay. "You're right! But let me finish. I found a bunch of rafts dumped in one corner—most were in good condition, while a few were beyond repair. I also found a lot of industrial-grade adhesive tape lying around."

"Now I need to check one more thing," he continued, pulling out a hammer and chisel from their toolbox, a hint of doubt in his voice that he hoped to clear up.

"Before I break this brick, I want you all to see something," he said, pointing to a scorpion symbol embossed on the lateral side of the brick.

Vicky pulled out his spy camera and clicked a few photos. Tej placed the brick on a flat surface and began chiseling away at it with careful precision. Each tap of the chisel echoed softly in the silence around them, while the others watched with great curiosity.

Vivek picked up the camera and started recording the whole chiseling effort. As he was tapping gently and clearing off the debris, they suddenly noticed something shining!

"Gold!" everyone exclaimed in a hushed tone.

With just a few more taps, Tej had a solid gold bar weighing approximately over a hundred grams in his hand!

"That's pretty much what I expected!" Tej whispered to the other team members.

Tej turned to Vicky, a spark of excitement in his eyes. "Do you remember the brick I picked up at the factory, which James had objected to? Well, I found it to be much heavier than a usual brick used in construction. That's when I began to question myself about what was so special about it. Why is it built with a different specification? Why is it so heavy? It just didn't make any sense to me then. I also noticed the scorpion mark on that brick, the same which we saw on this one."

"Remember our visit to the railway station? I asked you to come along because I wanted to check if those bricks were different from the brick I picked up at the factory. When I examined the bricks in the truck, they were lighter and seemed like any ordinary construction brick. None of them had the scorpion mark embossed on them," he continued.

Vicky replied with excitement and relief, "So now it's clear! The bricks transported by Pedro's trucks and then by train to various construction sites are normal bricks meant for construction, while these 'scorpion grade' bricks with gold bars inside never take that route! Does this mean the bricks are strapped to the rafts and dumped into the water, only to be collected downstream by someone and stored in the cabin we discovered? And all of this happens in rough weather so that anyone watching from the near side of the lake won't have a clear view of what's going on."

"Yes! And the rafts kept the bricks afloat for easy retrieval!" Tej said. "That also explains the sounds of something dropping in the water that we heard."

"And that's supposed to be the handiwork of the headless boatman!" Vicky chuckled. "Now we know why he shows up on rainy, stormy nights—for smuggling gold in secret! Since when ghosts developed a taste for gold?"

"He is not doing this alone! There are others involved for sure!" Tej remarked. "I think everything connects so well now, Vicky! Also, switching off the lantern could be a signal to the person waiting below the waterfall that the bricks are on the way! This also took care that the boat is not noticed as it drops the goods and makes its way back to the cave. The fog generated from the boat was yet another method to divert attention so that they could send the bricks downstream and make a quick dash back to the cave."

"And to create that spooky atmosphere and scare everyone away!" Vicky added. "That way, the boatman and his accomplices ensured that no one dared to come close and investigate."

"Ah, that's the reason why we couldn't spot the boat on camera after the fog cleared! It was already in the cave by that time!" Tanmay said. He felt a wave of relief, realizing that Anna might not be a ghost after all. The clues were coming together, easing his worries.

"Correct," Tej confirmed.

"You mean the boatman generated the fog artificially?" Tukya asked.

"Hundred percent! You get fogger machines of different types today! That's no big deal," Vicky said.

Tanmay was not entirely convinced. "What about the headless boatman? How can a human be headless and alive? How is that possible?"

"That's probably the last piece of the puzzle. Ghosts only haunt or scare people; they don't smuggle gold!" said Tej. "Well, Tanmay, you questioned us on your role, right? Here is where it starts! Be prepared!"

Tanmay turned to Vivek and Tukya for their reassurance.

"We're all set!" the team replied, their voices unwavering, brimming with confidence. They were ready for whatever lay ahead.

14

Final Showdown

A few days passed, and the weather was nice and clear once again. Then came the day they were waiting for! Clouds started building again, which raised the team's hopes.

"We are in for some rain tonight! time to meet Anna!" Vicky and Tej exclaimed.

By ten o'clock at night, it had started to drizzle. Vicky and Tej reminded Tanmay and the team of their roles one more time before hopping onto their mountain bikes and racing downhill with lightning speed! The mud road down the hill was slippery and rough, but the Kamat brothers skillfully navigated it, staying steady and maintaining a fast pace. They couldn't afford to lose any more time—this was their chance to catch the headless boatman, and they were already behind schedule. The road was challenging, but they pushed on, determined not to miss their chance.

Chatur couldn't be convinced to stay back this time; he galloped after them, keeping pace with their mountain bikes.

Reaching their usual spot, the Kamat brothers hid their bikes before slipping into the water, snorkels on. They swam underwater, careful to breathe through their snorkels and stay out of sight. Chatur followed closely behind, his sleek, dark fur blending perfectly with the shadows of the night—no snorkel needed for him!

Once they reached the cave's entrance, they swam to the shallow area and got out of the water onto the jetty, and so did Chatur. He paused for a moment, and then gave himself a vigorous shake-off, sending droplets flying in every direction.

"No one seemed to be around!" Tej exclaimed and signaled to Vicky to move inside the cave.

They jumped onto the jetty and sneaked into the boat cabin. Chatur stayed back to keep watch and provide cover for them.

Inside the cabin, they could see four rafts. Stacks of bricks were tightly sealed in waterproof containers and strapped to the rafts with the help of industry grade adhesive tapes, and a large fogger machine was tucked in a corner!

"Just what we thought! Perfectly matches our theory!" Vicky whispered.

The Kamat brothers had kept the communication on. "Tanmay, can you hear us?" Tej whispered.

Tanmay replied, "Yes Sir!" This time, he spoke in a lower tone, being mindful of his eardrums.

They moved closer to the neatly packed bricks and noticed the scorpion mark! Vicky quickly took out the spy camera and snapped a few pictures, eager to gather evidence at every opportunity. After a moment, he swiftly tucked the camera back into his pocket, keeping it safe.

A few minutes went by. "Surprisingly, there is no one around to guard the cargo," Tej said.

"There they are!" They heard a loud voice from behind.

Just as they were about to turn and see who it was, something struck them hard on the head.

Both fell on the cabin floor with a thud! Whatever hit them had knocked them down into a sub-conscious state.

"Tie them up! Make sure they don't escape!" A man with a rough, loud voice instructed his henchmen.

The satellite communication was still active, and Tanmay and his friends heard every word clearly. A sudden chill ran down their spine—They sensed something was off! Without wasting a second, they sprang into action.

They rushed to the satellite phone and sent out an SOS message to the Coast Guard. Vivek pulled out his phone and alerted the local police.

They were doing exactly as directed by Tej and Vicky. Although they did what they were supposed to, they felt tense. They were tempted to grab the revolver and other weapons and head for the boat to defend their friends.

But then they recalled the clear instructions from the Kamat brothers: They were not supposed to leave their post. All they could do was pray and hope for the best.

Restless but with no option to leave, their eyes were glued to the MacBook screen and their ears were focused on the satellite phone, eagerly waiting to hear back from the Coast Guard.

Back at the boat, Tej and Vicky could sense someone splashing water on their faces. As they regained consciousness, they could see the headless boatman right in front of them!

Their hands were tied behind their backs. They struggled to break free, but their efforts were in vain.

This boatman was no ghost. He was someone who was wearing a long, huge white outfit with a bandhgala (a closed-neck suit). He had his face covered by a well-designed Halloween prop, which appeared to be a neck, with the head missing. A streak of blood trickled down on one side of the neck. The prop appeared to be custom designed for the boatman. It covered his entire head area perfectly, a prop that could have fooled anyone from a distance.

"So that's the reason why his entire head area appeared to be the neck from a distance," Tej whispered.

"Designer neck! Perfect fit! And the blood—ketchup, is it?" Vicky whispered back, unable to resist his sarcastic nature, or his craving for food.

They could see two distinct holes in the prop through which the boatman could see them. Next to him stood two assistants, while a third person, presumably the boat's driver, stood behind them.

The headless boatman overheard their whispers and growled, "That's red paint!" he scoffed, gesturing toward the blood. "But knowing that won't do you any good. You won't live to tell anyone what you saw! We warned you—several times! You didn't listen! You could have enjoyed your vacation peacefully and left us alone. We had no intention of harming you, but now you've left us with no choice!" he thundered, glaring down at them, his hands planted firmly on his hips.

The voice sounded so familiar, as if they had heard it before and knew the person hiding behind the prop, but they couldn't figure out who.

The team could hear everything on the other end of the communication system. Tanmay and Tukya picked up the satellite phone once again and sent out another SOS to the Coast Guard and the police.

"SOS! SOS!" they shouted over the phone. "The situation is getting worse! Please get here as quickly as possible. It's an emergency! Lives are at stake!" They tried to be as clear as possible.

They were extremely nervous! Every minute passing by felt like an hour!

After a few minutes, they heard a crackling voice on the satellite receiver. "We are on our way!" The Coast Guard's message came through clearly. "We will be there in about ten minutes!" In the background, the steady whir of helicopter blades suggested they were almost ready for takeoff.

"That's a relief," Vivek hoped. "I just wish they reach on time in this rough weather."

Back at the boat, the boatman turned to one of his assistants and ordered him. "Leave them here for now! We will throw them overboard once our boat reaches the waterfall. They will have no chance of surviving. They will be almost dead after they fall over. The leopards below the waterfall are in for a late-night party! They will drag them deep into the forest, never to be found!"

The headless boatman and his assistants left the boat.

"This boatman, whoever he is, won't start the boat until there is heavy downpour," Tej whispered.

Vicky glanced back and nodded in agreement. They both knew they had some time on their hands, as they could only sense a light drizzle from their current position.

Just then Chatur jumped into the boat and without wasting any time, started gnawing at the ropes. Moments later, Tej and Vicky were free. He started licking their faces.

"Chatur! Stop! There is no time for playing around. Good job! Now go outside the boat and hide!" Vicky said. "Make sure they don't spot you!"

Chatur responded with a mild howl and darted out of the boat as instructed. Tej and Vicky put their hands behind their backs and pretended as if they were still tied up. They kept their faces blank, hoping to maintain the act until the right moment to make their move.

The boatman entered the cabin once again along with his henchmen. It had started pouring. The Kamat brothers could hear heavy rain from inside the cabin.

"Say your last prayers, Kamat brothers! In just a few minutes, you'll either be sinking to your watery grave… or becoming the leopard's feast!" he declared, his voice booming with menace. Though they couldn't see his face, they could hear the cruel delight in his voice. "And if you're hoping for a last wish, I'm afraid I can't grant you that. I don't have the time… nor the patience. Ha ha ha!"

He then looked at the driver and ordered him, "Start the boat!" The driver quickly jumped into the driver's seat and took control.

Soon the boat was out of the cave. The headless boatman sat at the rear of the boat with the lantern while his assistants switched on the fogger. As soon as it reached the middle of the lake, the driver turned off the engine. He switched off the lantern, got up from his seat, and he, along with his henchmen, entered the cabin to dispose of the cargo and to throw the Kamat brothers overboard.

Without wasting any time, Tej lunged at the boatman and tackled him to the cabin floor.

Vicky decided to take on the assistants. With a swift punch, one of them fell into the water. He quickly followed up with an uppercut to the other assistant's chin, knocking him out instantly!

The driver, panicked, jumped out of the boat and began swimming back to the cave, while the assistant, who had initially fallen overboard after receiving Vicky's powerful punch, managed to climb back in. Exhausted and battered, he had no energy left to fight and collapsed.

The boatman reached out for his revolver in his pocket, but alert Chatur leaped from nowhere and clamped down his hand with his strong teeth!

"Aaaah!" the boatman yelled! He was in deep pain! The revolver fell out of his hand, clattering to the floor, as he tried to shake off Chatur. His strong canines had fractured his wrist.

"The ghost who yells!" Vicky chuckled.

"Chatur!" Tej exclaimed, his face lighting up with surprise. They were overjoyed to see him. He had sneaked back into the boat just in time; how could he leave Tej and Vicky alone?

Seeing their attention move to Chatur, boatman got back on his feet, ready to attack Tej and bring him down!

Tej caught the movement out of the corner of his eye. He quickly turned and landed two powerful punches on the boatman's decorative prop in rapid succession, striking the face hiding behind it.

Chatur leaped and grabbed the boatman's calf just as he crashed onto the neatly stacked brick cases, which were fastened to the rafts.

Tej then instructed Chatur, "Guard!" and picked up the revolver.

Chatur understood him loud and clear! He stood firmly in front of the boatman in his most frightful avatar. He did not allow him to bulge. His ferocious face, snarling teeth, and growls resembled nothing less than a baby werewolf ready to pounce.

Any movement, and the boatman would have fallen victim to Chatur's strong canines. He certainly didn't want the dog to have another go at him! He had enough!

"Halloween party over Mr. Boatman!" Vicky declared loudly.

"They should have arrived by now," Tej said. "The 'Observation Deck' should have sent an SOS a long time ago, but there's still no sign of the chopper!"

Moments later, the roar of whirling chopper blades filled the air. The chopper's spinning blades churned the lake water, sending out large waves too powerful for the boat to handle! It rocked violently as the chopper stood still right over it. It was the Indian Coast Guard!

The boatman and his henchmen, still regaining their senses, wondered what was going on!

"They are here! Perfect timing!" Tej exclaimed. "Our team has done its job!"

Vicky looked at him with a wide grin on his face.

"This is the Indian Coast Guard! We have you surrounded! You are within easy range of our snipers. One wrong move and you will be dead ducks!" The voice echoed through the chopper's loudspeaker, sharp and menacing, cutting through the heavy rain and howling winds. At the same time, the chopper's blinding spotlight shone directly on the boat, ensuring it was locked onto their radar, leaving no chance of escape.

Tanmay, Vivek, and Tukya were watching all this on the MacBook screen from the 'Observation Deck'. They were all smiles!

They could hear Tej on their satellite phone receiver, "Team! Can you hear us? Well Done! Mission Accomplished!"

"Loud and clear! Thank God you are safe and sound! See you soon!" Tanmay shouted in excitement, which sent his ears ringing once again. Tej could hear Tukya and Vivek cheering and clapping in the background!

The boatman and his crew surrendered without a fight, knowing they were no match for the Indian Coast Guard.

They stepped out of the cabin one after the other, hands raised in the air, offering no resistance. Everyone was lifted into the chopper using a suspended ladder.

The Coast Guard ensured they picked up the driver, who was making a futile attempt to reach the cave. Realizing that his team had already been arrested, he clutched the flexible ladder dropped from the chopper and climbed aboard.

As the chopper approached the village, the Kamat brothers could see the entire village gathered on the banks of the lake down below. Some had umbrellas, while others were drenched in the relentless rain, which showed no signs of stopping.

Everyone watched the action unfold from the lake promenade, unfazed by the rain. To them, it felt like a live James Bond action scene—only the background music was missing.

Final Showdown

Vicky requested the Coast Guard, "Please send out a message to the police to direct the villagers to the community hall. We will present our findings over there."

15

The Unmasking Ceremony

*I*t was about 5 o'clock in the morning by the time the entire operation concluded. The Coast Guard chopper made a landing in an open space where the police were waiting to receive them. The boatman and his henchmen were handed over and forced into a police truck.

"Let's take them to the community hall," Tej requested the police inspector. The police had directed the villagers there and were already waiting when the Kamat brothers arrived.

At the community hall, prominent figures from the village, including the Panchayat heads and elders, were seated right in front, facing the Kamat brothers. Notable personalities, such as Mr. Vilasrao Patil and Pedro occupied a row just behind them, followed by some villagers. The rest had to stand outside, as the hall was too small to accommodate everyone.

All were eagerly waiting for a glimpse of the headless boatman. The villagers were growing restless, their voices rising in a chorus of frustration and anticipation. They shouted in anger, demanding: "Show us the headless boatman! Reveal his true face! Unmask the monster!" The tension in the air was thick as they anxiously waited for what would happen next.

The police dragged the handcuffed headless boatman to the center of the community hall and forced him into one of the chairs.

His other accomplices were still in the police truck outside, kept under heavy guard to protect them from the likely anger of the crowd, who could easily turn violent. Once the room settled, the police inspector stepped forward, reaching for the mask that concealed the boatman's face.

With a swift tug, he pulled it away, revealing the man behind the disguise.

The crowd fell silent for a moment, their eyes wide in shock. "It's James!" the villagers gasped, their voices a mix of disbelief and horror. How could it be him? Sitting there, right in front of them. There was pin-drop silence in the hall!

Pedro just couldn't keep his cool. He erupted, "James! You!... After everything I've done for you all these years, is this how you repay me? I was nurturing a criminal! I can't believe this!"

James hung his head, looking ashamed. "I was told we were doing this for the village's good," he said quietly.

"For the village's good?" one of the villagers shouted, clearly angry. "What good is this, James? You've made us live in fear all these years!"

The room grew louder with voices, all filled with anger. "Did we ask you to cause all this trouble?" another villager yelled. "Why did you do it, James? Why betray us?"

James didn't move, his face pale. He sat there, silent, as the questions kept coming.

An elder in the room stood up slowly. His voice was firm, but calm. "You're not smart enough to plan all of this," he said. "Tell us, James—who told you to do this? Who do you work for? Who is behind all of this?"

James hesitated, shifting uncomfortably. After a brief pause, he finally spoke, his voice shaky. "Vilasrao Patil Saheb!" he stammered, looking at Mr. Patil with fear and hoping for support.

The villagers lost their temper. "What! How could you drag our Patil Saheb into this! How dare you take his name! He is like a God to us!" they shouted.

Vicky stepped in to simmer things down. "Please! Please calm down! Give us some time. We will present the entire case to you all." he requested the villagers.

Over a hundred villagers were witnessing the unbelievable. There was a real chance for things to go out of control. Just a few coast guards and a dozen policemen weren't enough to handle such a large crowd.

The Kamat brothers rushed into one of the adjoining rooms in the community hall for a brief preparation.

The Coast Guard whisked James away to join his partners in crime. The villagers stayed back, waiting for the Kamat brothers to return, unwilling to leave without knowing the complete picture.

16

Connecting the Dots

The Kamat brothers helped themselves with a quick cup of coffee sponsored by Vivek's Café as they worked on their MacBook.

Chatur was hungry after the eventful night — he had played a starring role in the evening's adventure! Vivek made sure he was served a large bowl full of pedigree and water. It was a well-deserved feast for the brave Belgian Malinois.

After some time, they returned to the main hall. Among other gadgets, they had a portable projector with them. They focused it on one of the plain whitewashed walls of the community hall.

Tej set up everything, and Vicky took the lead to start the presentation while Chatur sat beside them.

"Let me start from the day we arrived in Ganeshpuri for our vacation," he began.

They projected some selfies taken while Tanmay was showing them around the village—some by the lake, others atop the hill near the temple. In a few of them, Pravin had inadvertently been captured in the background.

"Can you spot Pravin in the background of most of these selfies?" Vicky asked, scanning the room.

A few villagers nodded in agreement.

"Just for those who don't know, Pravin is a factory worker at Pedro's Brick Factory. When we realized that he was trailing us, it was obvious that someone was interested in keeping a watch on us, and Pravin was likely the one assigned to keep tabs on us," Vicky continued.

He informed the villagers how they decided to spend a few days camping on the hilltop below the temple area to monitor the far side of the lake.

Tej interjected, "Our suspicions turned into certainty after events of our first evening at the camp. Someone was watching us from behind the thick bushes, a few meters away from our tent. Just as Chatur sniffed him out and alerted us, he ran away, and while doing so," he paused, turning to pick up the evidence bag containing the shoe, which he displayed to the villagers. "One of his shoes came off. Upon closer examination, we noticed some clay residue on the sole."

"It's a left-foot shoe," Vicky pointed out. "The next afternoon, we visited Pedro's brick factory," he continued.

"During the factory tour, amongst other things related to brick manufacturing, we learned that clay is one of the key materials used in the process. We suspected that the shoe must belong to someone who works there."

"Again, at the factory, we noticed Pravin limping," Vicky continued, capturing the audience's undivided attention. "When Tanmay inquired about the injury, James quickly intervened and told us that Pravin had twisted his foot while working at the factory. Pravin could have spoken for himself!"

"He had bruises on his left foot in several places, while his right foot was perfectly normal—an injury that doesn't happen from a simple twist. This led us to confirm it was Pravin watching us, and he got these injuries while running barefoot, wearing only one shoe on his right foot, the previous evening."

"That also made us wonder if James was trying to cover up something," Tej interjected, his eyes narrowing as he spoke.

Tej continued, "There was one more thing that we noticed at Pedro's factory. One of the bricks I picked up was noticeably heavier than the standard bricks used for construction. I saw that brick embossed with a scorpion mark."

Vicky quickly displayed a photo of the brick with the scorpion mark as Tej spoke.

"Additionally, James had no reason to react the way he did, which solidified his position on the suspect list," Tej explained to the villagers how he had behaved when he picked up the brick to inspect it.

Pedro was shocked to hear all this. He couldn't contain himself, "All this! Happening in my factory! My most trusted man, doing all…"

Tej glanced at Pedro, nodded, and interrupted him. "Mr. Pedro, most of the bricks manufactured in your factory are perfectly fine—I've examined them myself. You or your factory wasn't the problem; it was being used for something illegal, right under your nose."

He then explained to the villagers how he had inspected the bricks ready for dispatch on one of Pedro's trucks at the train station and found nothing wrong with them. They didn't have the scorpion mark embossed on them.

"One more thing to note about Pedro's factory was his nephew Andrew's warehouse. In the warehouse, among other equipment, we saw numerous rafts in deflated condition. When Pedro mentioned that he provides training on Adventure Sports somewhere far from the village, we couldn't help but wonder why he stored all the equipment so far from the actual training location," Vicky added.

"Wait! There's more!" Tej took over; his tone serious, as he prepared to share additional details.

He quickly played the video clips captured by the camera they had installed alongside the road leading to the cave. The footage clearly showed Mr. Vilasrao Patil approaching the cave, engaging in conversation with someone, and then retracing his steps along the same route on several occasions!

The Kamat brothers wanted to ensure the villagers saw the proof for themselves before casting Mr. Patil in a negative light. They were cautious of provoking another violent reaction from the villagers.

"Mr. Patil will need to explain what he was doing out there in the cave late at night. James might have lied, but the cameras didn't! Am I right, Mr. Patil?" Tej concluded.

The villagers remained calm, but disbelief surrounded them. They were thoroughly confused, struggling to process what they had just witnessed.

"Look, we do not know yet if Mr. Patil is involved. And if he is, to what extent! Please be with us till the very end," Tej said.

Vicky stepped in to update the villagers on how they cycled to the banks of the lake on the far side and swam across to see the headless boatman up close.

"When we spotted the boatman from a short distance in his boat, we initially believed the ghost to be real. The entire scene was so frightening that it could have caused anyone a heart attack," he said.

As Vicky spoke, Tej clicked a few close-up photos of the headless boatman to display on the projector screen. The entire audience was taken aback. Despite knowing that Anna's ghost wasn't real anymore, the pictures were undeniably scary, evoking a sense of unease that sent chills down their spines.

"We mustered all our courage and decided to stay back and observe. After a while, we heard several splashes, as if something heavy had been dropped into the water. Unfortunately, we couldn't see what had fallen, as it occurred on the other side of the boat. Once the boat returned to the cave, we took a deep dive into the lake to investigate what it was."

"When we couldn't find anything, we speculated that it might be part of the haunting. If someone were playing tricks on us, the only possibility was that they had pushed whatever they dropped over the waterfall for someone to retrieve it downstream."

Tej stepped in, saying, "The following night we ventured into the area at the base of the waterfall and discovered a small cabin not too far away. Inside, we found worn-out rafts and large rolls of strong adhesive tape in a cabin located further from the waterfall the next day. We also discovered several bricks embossed with the same scorpion mark!"

"That was when we envisioned the possibility that the bricks were sealed in waterproof containers and strapped to the rafts to make them float, allowing for easy retrieval."

Vicky displayed the photos of the bricks, neatly sealed in waterproof containers and strapped to the rafts in the boat's cabin as Tej spoke.

"But why would anyone send bricks over the waterfall? And sealed in containers? It doesn't make any sense to me," one of the young villagers inquired.

"Smart observation!" Vicky exclaimed. "You will have your answer in a few minutes. Watch carefully!"

Tej played the video captured when the brick was chiseled out while the audience glued their eyes on it.

"We brought one brick back with us and chiseled it out," he continued.

The tapping echoed through the hall as the video played on, and soon, a streak of yellow appeared—it was glittering metal!

"Gold!" some villagers exclaimed as a large gold ingot was uncovered from inside the ordinary construction brick.

"Yes! Gold! Gold Smuggling!" Tej exclaimed. "The scorpion bricks proved to be excellent camouflage! Andrew fooled the police for years! Who on earth would have thought of checking construction bricks?"

"This explains how Andrew was using the rafts stored at the warehouse. The Adventure Sports training and certification were just a cover to throw people off. Those pictures in the warehouse were all fake, meant to mislead his uncle Pedro," he added.

Just then, the police inspector stepped in and announced, "We've arrested Andrew. He was caught trying to flee in a red Lamborghini, carrying bricks from his cabin. He is now in custody, and we're investigating his potential connections with robbers and black marketeers. We suspect he was acquiring stolen or smuggled gold at negotiated rates and reselling it elsewhere. Rest assured, we'll uncover the full story soon!"

The inspector then turned to the Kamat brothers and added, "Thank you for your timely tip-off—it helped us apprehend him just in time."

"Oh! Red Lamborghini! Now we know who was trying to hurt us, Tej!" Vicky exclaimed.

Chatur responded with a loud, booming bark followed by a low growl, causing everyone to burst into laughter.

His bark helped lighten the atmosphere a bit. He recalled the Lamborghini incident, which had left his friends with bruises.

Vicky stepped in and requested James be brought back to the community hall for interrogation. He also requested a guilty-looking Mr. Patil not to leave the hall.

"The story is not over yet! We still have some dots to connect and show you the complete picture," he said to the villagers.

The police dragged James into the community hall once again.

Tej turned to Mr. Patil. "Sir, do you have anything to say? James has accused you, but as one of the main suspects, his testimony carries little weight. However, what about these videos? They clearly show you!"

Mr. Patil chose to remain silent.

"But these pictures don't lie, do they?" Tej pressed, his stern gaze locked onto Mr. Patil. "You can't deny your involvement. Sooner or later, the truth will come out! Your silence will only indicate that you are part of this—that you accept what James said about you earlier... that you're the one behind it all!"

It was true that Mr. Patil was their good friend's father, and they were staying at his house, receiving the best hospitality, but none of this swayed them. They were professionals, committed to their duty, and refused to show any leniency toward him.

The villagers were confused and began to murmur among themselves, creating a chaotic atmosphere.

"Silence, please," Vicky shouted. "Please! Just be quiet!" The villagers calmed down once again resulting in pin-drop silence in the hall.

Mr. Vilasrao Patil paused for a while. He asked for some water and then started to talk. He could not hold himself back anymore.

"I will tell you everything," he said in a low tone. He took a deep breath and began to speak, "I know I have wronged you all!" He raised his head, looked at the villagers, and continued in an apologetic tone. "But I did all this for the village. Although our backyard farms and fishing activity provided for our day-to-day survival, all of us here know that the real money came from the homestay business."

All the villagers nodded in agreement, eager to hear him out. Despite being the suspect, a deep respect for Mr. Patil still lingered in their hearts.

"Over the years, we saw the number of tourists dropping. Repeat business nearly disappeared. People started moving out of the village in search of better opportunities. I knew the village would soon be deserted, and I had to save it from extinction," he continued.

"I came up with this ghost story based on an incident that happened about fifty years ago. I convinced James to play the ghost. The story spread like wildfire! It was an instant hit! We started getting tourists again on weekends, all eager to spot Anna's ghost. Many camped overnight hoping for a glimpse of the headless boatman. Photography and videography were strictly forbidden to maintain secrecy. We told the tourists it would anger Anna's spirit. They were provided with binoculars only," he added.

He turned to Tanmay and said, "But I was never in this gold smuggling business, son! I have never done anything illegal in my life."

On hearing Mr. Patil's confess, James mustered some courage and began to speak, "Andrew somehow learned about the headless boatman drama. He left out Patil Saheb as he was a prominent personality in the village and lacked the courage to confront him. Since I was the weaker one with no influence, he threatened to expose me and forced me to assist him on this gold smuggling racket. I had no choice! I was framed! Please have mercy on me!" he tried to play the victim card.

The villagers were thoroughly shocked to hear Mr. Vilasrao's confession. This was too much for them to digest in a single day.

Just then, one of the elderly villagers stood up and said, "I do agree that we've seen an increase in tourists ever since the ghost was spotted, but at the same time, it had put the entire village in a grip of fear. Cafés and other businesses near the lake had started closing early."

Pedro was devastated after hearing all this. He covered his face with his hands in disgust. First James, and now Andrew, were involved in the shoddy ghost business, with his factory being the epicenter. He chose to remain silent, unsure of what to say.

Tanmay lashed out at his father. "Baba, why did you choose the wrong path? Was this necessary? You've thrown away your reputation! How will Ma and I face the villagers now? How will we live in this village? Having someone play a ghost to fool people is also a kind of fraud! I'm utterly ashamed of your actions. And as for people leaving the village for better opportunities—there were other ways to address that problem!"

This was followed by complete silence in the community hall.

Just then one of the villagers stood up and questioned Tej. "But how did the coast guard come to know?"

"Our father works for the Indian Intelligence Wing. We made sure to update him on our progress daily. Since this was our first case, we didn't want to miss out on his experience. He advised us that the easiest way to catch the headless boatman red-handed in the middle of a huge lake was to send out a helicopter. He coordinated with the coast guard. And yes, it was Tanmay and his friends who tipped them off at the right time!" Tej said.

"I have a question," one of the villagers asked in a tense voice. "What happened to the tourists? Were they killed? How did they vanish without a trace?"

James was quick to defend himself, "Look! I admit we have been running this gold smuggling racket, but I swear we have not killed anyone! I know nothing about the tourists."

Tej interjected, "Well, but you were planning to throw us overboard to the leopards, weren't you? You have criminal tendencies. You will be questioned by the police. You are not getting away easily!"

Tej then turned to the villager who brought up the question of the missing tourists and said, "We have everything covered in detail in our dossier that we will submit later today to the police."

"I am certain the case will be reopened. I'm very sorry we completely missed updating you on the tourists. Thank you for bringing it to our attention!" he apologized to the villager.

Tej and Vicky looked around to check if someone had any further questions. "Any more questions?" they asked, looking around.

They paused for a minute, waiting to see if anyone else had something to ask.

"That's it, then! No more questions. Case solved!" the Kamat brothers declared triumphantly. "If anyone has further questions, they can request a certified copy of our dossier from the police—it has all the answers."

The villagers clapped in appreciation! They thanked and congratulated the Kamat brothers once again as they packed their belongings and walked out of the community hall!

The police arrested Mr. Patil and took him away along with James.

For Tanmay, it was the worst day of his life. The Kamat brothers expected him to be very upset at them; after all, they were the reason behind his Baba's arrest. But to their surprise, though, he seemed to be calm and composed.

"Guys, you don't have to feel awkward. You did what you had to. You just exposed the truth. The fact that my Baba is involved in all this isn't your fault," he said coolly.

"Tanmay, we're planning to stay for the first hearing at the district court. We don't want to leave you alone in this situation," Tej said, his voice filled with concern. "I truly believe the court will grant your Baba a lighter sentence. Even though his methods were wrong, I think his intentions were noble. He's neither a smuggler nor a murder suspect. We're here for you, and we'll face this together."

Tanmay nodded, holding onto that hope, a sense of relief washing over him. He felt a little better after hearing Tej's comforting words.

As they walked back home together, Tanmay looked at Tej and Vicky, feeling both grateful and heavy-hearted. "I don't know what to say… but thank you for being here with me," he said quietly.

17
Goodbye Ganeshpuri!

A couple of days later, the first hearing at the district court concluded. James, Andrew, and their accomplices were taken into custody. The case of the missing tourists was reopened and assigned to the local police.

The court could not find any fraudulent transactions in Mr. Patil's bank account. They were not able to link him to the gold smuggling racket either.

They considered his past deeds and all the social activities he had done for the village, which outweighed this one mistake he made. The court granted him bail with a fine of one lakh rupees. The judge released him with a warning, instructing him not to travel outside his village without the court's permission until the case was closed.

After reaching the village, Mr. Patil apologized to the Kamat brothers. "Boys, I'm sorry that all of this started because of me. But thank you for exposing this entire smuggling racket. If you hadn't come here, we would have never known."

The villagers had made up their minds to forgive Mr. Patil and welcomed him back with open arms. They arrived with a music band, a huge garland, and a large box of sweets to celebrate his return.

"We want to erase the past few days from our hearts, Patil Saheb, and make a fresh start! You are our leader and will always remain our leader!" they declared warmly.

Mr. Patil's eyes glistened with emotion as he addressed them. "I've learned my lesson. Let's work together to make Ganeshpuri a village people won't want to leave. It's time to explore new livelihoods beyond homestays and fishing. We will make it happen!"

The villagers erupted in applause. They knew Mr. Patil was a man of his word and felt confident he would bring about the change.

Tanmay and his mother felt a sense of relief as they watched the villagers accept Mr. Patil, signaling that their lives were gradually returning to normal.

The next day, a small felicitation function was held at the community hall. The Panchayat members, Mr. Vilasrao, Pedro, and a few others thanked the Kamat brothers, Tanmay, and his team for unraveling the mystery behind the headless boatman.

They presented the Kamat brothers with richly embroidered shawls and a stunning marble replica of the Ganesha idol from the Ganeshpuri temple, intricately carved with remarkable detail. The gift was a symbol of their deep gratitude and respect.

Tanmay, Vivek, and Tukya were honored with gleaming medals, for their bravery and contribution.

A special glittering medal and a huge hamper full of delicious cookies from Vivek's Cafe were presented to Chatur as well!

He trotted onto the stage proudly and accepted it happily with a big woof! He deserved it! The applause grew louder, as he had become everyone's favorite by now!

It wasn't his first recognition. He had received many gallantry awards before while serving his country.

After the function, the entire village then escorted them to their Mahindra Thar. It was time for the Kamat brothers to bid farewell to the village.

"Do visit us again!" the villagers exclaimed.

"We certainly will!" the Kamat brothers replied, accepting the invitation. "But next time, we are hoping for peaceful vacation; no more headless boatmen!"

Laughter erupted amongst the villagers as they hoped this was their first and last encounter with a ghost.

The Kamat brothers bid goodbye by waving out to the villagers as they hopped onto their Mahindra Thar and drove away.

Chatur was already on the backseat. He was thrilled to have the entire back seat to himself once again!

Soon, they were back on the winding roads of the Konkan Ghats. Surprisingly, most of the potholes had been patched up, making the drive much smoother than they had anticipated!

Tej asked, "So, what next?"

"Well, back to college to answer our final semester exams, and who knows, another adventure may be around right after that!" Vicky replied.

Tej's iPhone started ringing. It was their dad! As Tej was driving, he handed over the iPhone to Vicky. He put it on speaker.

"Hello papa!" both exclaimed.

"Congratulations to you both on cracking your first case! Ghostbusters, aren't you? Well, everyone at the department is calling you that!" Their dad chuckled, "Well, finish off your exams now and be ready for more! I have another case lined up for you."

"I will be there with your mother at your convocation ceremony! Or maybe I'll meet you right after the exams. I need you on this case as soon as possible," he continued.

"So, where's our next case, Papa?" Tej asked eagerly.

"I'll share the details when we meet, son. It's not appropriate to discuss such matters in detail over the phone. I've got a meeting coming up, so I need to go!" Nishant Kamat replied in a warm voice before hanging up.

"Another case?" Vicky exclaimed, glancing at Tej. "We are always ready, aren't we?" Tej said with a grin. "But yes, exams first!"

Chatur heard the entire conversation. He howled in excitement, eager to let the Kamat brothers know that he was on board!

The Kamat brothers laughed heartily as they navigated the winding roads of the Konkan Ghats.

www.ingramcontent.com/pod-product-compliance
Lightning Source LLC
LaVergne TN
LVHW041220080526
838199LV00082B/1341